DOCTOR WHO
THE TWIN DILEMMA

For Katia,
with fondest love

DOCTOR WHO
THE TWIN DILEMMA

Based on the BBC television serial by Anthony Steven by arrangement with the British Broadcasting Corporation

---

ERIC SAWARD

Number 103
in the Doctor Who Library

A TARGET BOOK
published by
the Paperback Division of
W.H. ALLEN & Co. PLC

A Target Book
Published in 1986
By the Paperback Division of
W.H. Allen & Co. PLC
44 Hill Street, London W1X 8LB

First published in Great Britain by
W.H. Allen & Co. PLC in 1985

Printed and bound in Great Britain by
Anchor Brendon Ltd, Tiptree, Essex

The BBC producer of *The Twin Dilemma* was
John Nathan-Turner, the director was Peter Moffatt

ISBN 0 426 20155 8

Contents

1

Home Time

The house stood on Lydall Street. It was part of a beautifully preserved Georgian terrace, its graceful façade as pleasing today as when it was first built in 1810, some five hundred years earlier. In fact, Lydall Street was the only Georgian terrace left standing in the metropolis. It was also the only street with houses built of brick. To the people who lived in the flameproof, plastic buildings of the city, Lydall Street had enormous charm, an incredible sense of history and a tactile quality missing from their own mirror-smooth, vinyl environment.

The reality of living there was, of course, quite different. The houses were draughty, uncomfortable and cost a fortune to maintain. Although it was an honour to be allowed to occupy such a dwelling, it was also vital that you were rich. Some people said it was better if you were mad. The truth was, of course, it was better if you were both.

The family who occupied number twenty-five possessed the above qualifications in great abundance. But they also possessed a much greater and more precious gift – genius. The Sylvest family, for it was they who occupied number twenty-five, were all gifted mathematicians.

Professor Archie Sylvest was a tall man with a grey, matted thatch of hair that wouldn't lie neatly however much it was combed. His face was florid and his waist thick from drinking too much Voxnic (a delicious alcoholic beverage made from fermented viston seeds). As it was again chic to be fat, and, as Voxnic was this season's most fashionable drink, Archie was able to pat his paunch with considerable pride as he ordered yet another round.

In fact, Archie should have been totally happy. His wife, Nimo, was a stimulating companion. He loved his work at the University. Wallowed in the company of his students. Revelled in the respect shown by his fellow lecturers. Loved drinking too much Voxnic with computer programmer Vestal Smith, a person of deep warmth, deep personal understanding and even deeper blue eyes. In fact, Archie would have been totally happy if it hadn't been for one thing: he was frightened to go home.

For there were his twin sons.

Romulus and Remus Sylvest were twelve year old identical twins. Such was their precise mirror image of each other, even their parents were occasionally confused. This gave the twins enormous pleasure and they would go out of their way to create even further embarrassment. The trouble was, they didn't know when to stop and they would go on and on and on. Their insistence verged on the psychotic. For a while Archie and Nimo wondered what the blending of their genes had created, but slowly, painfully, the truth emerged – the twins, like themselves, were gifted mathematicians. Unfortunately the genetic mix that had provided the twins with their talent did not cover other areas of their intellectual development. In many ways they were dumb. And when it came to emotional maturation, it had required several psychologists and a battery of complex tests to establish the evidence that there had been any. The truth was that their genius had done little to enhance them as human beings. Instead their gift sat on them like some congenital malformation, distorting the shape and symmetry of their personality. But unlike a club foot or a hunchback, which could be surgically corrected, their disfigurement had proved incurable. They would forever remain immature mischief-makers with the mathematical ability to destroy the universe.

Archie knew this and it terrified him. Nimo knew it too, and, like her husband, she had turned her back on the problem hoping it would go away. Archie coped by trying to swamp his responsibility in a sea of Voxnic in the company of computer programmer Vestal Smith. Nimo consumed her time a little more productively in the accumulation of academic degrees. But even she was beginning to wonder whether embarking on a fifth Ph.D was really a worthwhile way for a grown-up person to spend their time.

The house was quiet. Archie stared at the reflection of his tired face in the bathroom mirror and wondered whether there were any poisons that would defy the pathologist's skill. He found it therapeutic, while combing his hair, to plan the demise of his children. When Archie had first mentioned his macabre preoccupation to his psychiatrist, he had expected cries of outrage and despair, along with a prescription to raise his dose of Mestobam to five hundred milligrams per hour. But instead, the analyst had sighed, switched on an ancient recording of a Bartok string quartet, lit a cigarette and said, somewhat bored, 'Infanticide is a very common fantasy amongst the intelligentsia. In fact,' he continued, pausing only to fill his lungs with smoke, 'I only become worried when a patient *doesn't* harbour the desire to murder a close relation.'

Archie had felt horrified by this news. The thought that most of his friends and colleagues stalked the metropolis with murder in their hearts was one thing, but the revelation that his fantasy was *ordinary* induced a mental relapse requiring many months of deep and intensive analysis. It wasn't until a full year later that Archie felt able to return to the thoughts of murdering his children. This had been prompted by remarks his psychiatrist had made one dank winter morning, when Archie was feeling smugly at peace with the world.

'You know, Sylvest, your psyche has become lopsided,' the doctor had said, reaching for yet another of his specially made cigarettes. 'Your problem is that you lack feelings of guilt, anguish, turmoil.' He paused for a moment and blew a smoke ring. Archie watched, impressed by the psychiatrist's skill.

'You are too calm. Someone of your intellectual ability requires a damper, a neurosis, to complement the creative side of their personality.'

Archie had looked puzzled. He had spent a fortune having himself straightened out. Now the man who had helped him achieve his cheerful, contented disposition, was telling him he was *too* happy. *What does the fool mean*? Archie pondered, undecided whether to sue the doctor for malpractice, or simply punch him on the nose.

But before he could make up his mind, the psychiatrist had said, 'Your life is too cosy. You are far too gifted to spend your days regurgitating tried and tested facts to your students. Too dynamic to waste your evenings in front of the viddy-screen.' The doctor leant forward and stared directly into Archie's eyes. 'You are a theoretical mathematician. It is time you went back to your proper work!'

Poor Archie gazed at the tiny, ruptured blood vessels in the corneas of his accuser's eyes and knew that what had just been said was true. His feeling of well-being was a lie. Original thought had become alien to him. He had grown lazy, undisciplined. Archie's face sagged as feelings of guilt began to course through him once more.

'Feeling guilty isn't enough!' The doctor's voice stabbed at him .'You once told me you hated your children.' Archie nodded. 'Then do something about it! Negative neurosis eats at the very being of a person. Everyone hates their children, wife, mother or father for one reason or another. To want them dead is not enough. You must do something about it!'

The words echoed inside Archie's head as he wondered whether his analyst wasn't moonlighting for Murder Incorporated.

'Well . . .' said Archie, somewhat stiffly, 'you prescribe that I should kill my children?'

'No . . .' The psychiatrist slouched back in his chair. 'I want you to think positively about killing them. Imagining them dead isn't enough. In your mind, you must work out a way of committing the perfect murder.'

'And then?'

'And then you will have power over your fantasy. When that occurs, you will be able to control it. Turn it to work positively for you. You understand?'

Archie didn't.

'I know that you love your children, but you are also jealous of them. That's why you want them dead. But if in your mind you can also kill them, then you will have turned a negative neurosis into a positive one. By seeing your fantasy for what it is, you will come to understand your jealousy.'

Archie thought for a moment. 'But should I find a way of committing the perfect murder, and then decide to carry it out, what will happen?'

The psychiatrist smiled. 'If your crime is perfect, then no-one will know. But should you have made a mistake, then you will go to prison for the rest of your natural life . . . And I will lose a very lucrative client.'

Archie involuntarily reached for one of the doctor's cigarettes, lit it, then coughed. Although he hadn't understood what the analyst had said, it would give him a great deal to think about.

'You may go now,' said the doctor dismissively. 'I will see you the same time on Thursday.'

In front of his bathroom mirror, Archie continued to idly comb his hair. The conversation with his psychiatrist had taken place some months earlier. He still didn't fully understand what had been said and neither had he worked out a way of committing the perfect murder. Although his guilt had returned with a vengeance, and he still hated the twins, he had at least started to work again, which gave him a certain satisfaction. All in all, life had become much as it was a year ago, except for one thing: he had developed a taste for specially made cigarettes.

As usual, Archie's hair remained impervious to the activity of the comb and he gave up. Instead he set to work on a large blackhead he had been cultivating. As his stubby fingers pummelled and massaged the blocked pore, his concentration was interrupted by the bang of the front door. Nimo had gone out without saying goodbye to the twins. Archie knew this would cause offence and now dreaded to say goodnight to them himself.

The offending pore liberated, Archie slipped on his best evening jacket and glanced at himself in the mirror. Pleased with what he saw, he then made his way along the hall towards the twins' bedroom. Downstairs he could hear the gentle whirr of well-oiled machinery – the android babysitter had arrived. Archie smiled. He knew the twins hated androids. Androids had no sense of their own importance and therefore were impossible to embarrass. *It will drive them wild with frustration!* he thought.

As he approached the twin's room, he slowed his pace. His nerve was going. So it was with some trepidation he tapped on their bedroom door. Not waiting for them to reply, he pushed it open and entered.

Poor Archie wasn't very good at pretending. The smile that covered his face would have caused a cat to laugh. His mouth was twisted and strained and the muscles in his cheeks twitched with the effort of keeping his lips apart. The smile itself resembled a terrible razor slash, his red lips the open wound, the white teeth standing in for the exposed bone. 'Hallo, boys,' he said, attempting to maintain the smile. This made him sound like some tenth rate ventriloquist, the fixed smile preventing him from moving his lips and forming his words properly.

Romulus looked up from the book he was reading and cast an indifferent look at his father. 'You've been squeezing your blackheads,' he said at last. Archie's expression collapsed, his confidence shattered. 'I hope you've washed your hands. I don't want you touching me with bacteria-covered fingers.'

Archie opened his mouth to speak, but nothing came out. *I want to kill them!* he screamed – but he only shouted this inside his head. *I want to tear them limb from limb!* But out loud he muttered 'I've come to say goodnight.'

Neither one of his sons replied. Romulus returning to his book and Remus continuing to rummage in a large wooden toy box.

Archie tried to cheer himself up by telling the twins about the android babysitter, but they remained impassive. He then enquired what sort of day they had had and the twins related in minute, boring detail each tedious event. Archie then attempted to counter bore by telling them about the publisher's party he was about to attend, but omitted to say that afterwards he was having dinner with computer programmer Vestal Smith – when the Voxnic would flow like water and he would receive lots of the deep understanding she was so good at.

But then the inevitable happened, the question Archie had dreaded. It was made doubly unpleasant as it came in the middle of thinking about Vestal Smith.

'Where's Mother?'

Archie locked his fantasy away in a large box marked 'private' and turned towards his hateful son.

'Er . . . well, Remus,' he muttered. Archie hated using the twin's names in case he got them wrong. 'Well . . . to be honest . . . er . . . she's busy.'

'Does that mean she isn't talking to us?' Remus's tone was as pompous and as arrogant as a tax official having just discovered a double entry. 'Or has she already gone out without saying goodbye?'

Archie reluctantly nodded. The twins retorted with a scowl, then said together 'Abandoned again!' This speaking as one person always unnerved Archie. He was aware that identical twins sometimes possessed an uncanny rapport with each other and were often able to anticipate what the other was about to say, but Romulus and Remus were able to bring a rather unpleasant edge to the way they used this talent.

'You we forgive, Father . . . but not Mother.' Their dual intonation was like a terrible threat.

'I wish you would be kinder to your mother.' Archie was surprised at how stern he sounded. He then became afraid when the two advanced towards him. Standing shoulder to shoulder they stared up into his face, their own countenance hard and unyielding. 'Why?' they said together. 'Because mother happened to give birth to us, does that automatically grant her a place in our affections?'

Archie wasn't certain if the question was meant to be rhetorical or not, as they didn't give him time to answer.

'Respect must be earnt, Father. Mother is a fool! You know that! Do you wish us to respect a fool. You've always said the contrary.'

A fool? A fool! How can they think she's a fool, he screamed inside his head. *A woman who has four Ph.Ds and more degrees than any other person this side of Vebus Twelve! A fool!*

Romulus and Remus continued to stare up at their father. Archie wondered if they could hear every ranting thought in his head. *Well, I hope you can!* But out loud he said somewhat stiffly, 'Your mother is who she is whether you think her a fool or not. It's no excuse for poor manners and lack of concern.'

Archie braced himself for a savage riposte, but instead the twins turned away. 'As you wish, Father,' they said as one voice and then crossed to their computer terminals.

Archie was puzzled. *Why the sudden change of mood?* Cautiously he looked around the room expecting the worse sort of danger. The twins never gave up without a struggle. As a rule they would fight to the last shred and tatter of their argument.

Once more Archie's paranoia took flight. *Perhaps they've put a bomb in my personal transporter. Reprogrammed the android babysitter. At this very moment it's making its way silently up the stairs, its micro-circuitry throbbing with one command: KILL ARCHIE SYLVEST!*

'Goodnight, Father.' The tone was one of dismissal, not farewell.

Archie's racing mind jerked to a halt. 'Oh . . .' he said, sounding awkward and embarrassed as though he'd been asked a question to which he should have known the answer. 'Right . . . Goodnight, boys.' There was no reply.

Archie closed the twins' bedroom door behind him. His demeanour was that of a reprimanded schoolboy leaving a headmaster's study. He was angry with himself. They always made him feel like a fool, yet he was every inch their equal. Had he not been called the finest mathematician since Albert Einstein? When only twenty years old, had he not published his thesis, 'Pure Mathematics and its Relationship with the Square Root of Minus Three.' (Archie was the first person to calculate the square root of minus three, until then, a feat considered impossible.) Not only had it astounded the mathematical world, but his book had become a best seller. He had proven his ability. *I am a legend in the world of mathematics. I dominate my subject like a colossus! What have those hateful children done? Nothing!*

Dejectedly Archie shuffled along the hall and down the stairs. Although he was a champion, a genius, Emperor of the Parellelogram, he knew it was simply a matter of time before he was replaced on the winner's pedestal by the twins. The consumption of all the Voxnic in the world couldn't change that. The twins were too gifted for it not to happen. The trouble was Archie was too proud for it not to hurt. His psychiatrist was right: he was jealous of his own children.

The front door of twenty-five Lydall Street swung open and the portly frame of the greatest mathematician since Albert Einstein stepped out. The evening air was cold and Archie gave an involuntary shudder as it embraced him. As he turned to close the door, a gruff, hairy voice said, 'Are you Professor Archie Sylvest?'

Smiling, Archie turned to face his questioner. The owner of the voice was even more Neanderthal than expected. Archie stared blankly at the man and wondered who he could be.

Suddenly something powerful and hairy settled on Archie's arm. At first glance, it resembled an enormous tropical spider, but on closer examination it turned out to be a muscular hand. The grip tightened on Archie's podgy limb, causing him to flinch. 'I'm Reginald Smith,' the voice grunted, 'Vestal Smith's husband!'

As ink travels on blotting paper, so did a look of horror slowly spread across the mathematician's face. At the same moment he seemed to lose control of his jaw and his mouth dropped open to reveal a set of excellent teeth. Unless Archie could immediately get his hand on a knuckle duster, a large club or the experience of a dozen karate lessons he would soon require the extensive service of an orthodontist. But such rescue only comes in fantasies and the grip, now hardening on his arm, reminded him of the impending reality.

From any point of view, it had not been Archie's day.

2

The Maladjusted Time Lord

Deep in space, aboard the Doctor's TARDIS, things weren't an awful lot better. Regeneration had taken place, the event that is both a blessing and a scourge of the Time Lords of Gallifrey.

When a Time Lord is in danger of dying, his body grown too old to go on working properly, or, as one reported case has it, for reasons of vanity, a Time Lord is able to change his physical shape. This is brought about by a massive release of a hormone called *lindos*, which, at lightening speed, is transported around the body causing it cells to reform and realign themselves. Although much work has been done by genetic engineers on Gallifrey, the process still remains a random and, in some cases, rather an erratic one.

Some Time Lords are able to proceed through their allotted twelve regenerations with enormous grace and dignity, growing older and more handsome with each change of shape. Others leap about to a startling degree, finishing one regeneration a wise and noble elder, only to start the next a youthful, boastful braggart. This, needless to say, can cause enormous emotional and psychological upset. A good example of this was Councillor Verne.

It is said that he had regenerated into the most beautiful person ever to be seen on Gallifrey. As a rule, beauty earns little esteem on that planet, but Verne was so startling in his good looks that other Time Lords wanted to be seen in his company. Soon he had been elevated to the rank of Councillor by his rich and powerful admirers, but some said, perhaps jealously, that he was as stupid as he was beautiful. Whether that was true or not didn't alter the fact that he was totally unsuited to the world of politics. And it was this ineptitude that brought about his downfall.

The Council of Gallifrey had been in session for days. The motion under debate was a very delicate one. The Council was divided, but the faction who included those who had sponsored Verne's rapid rise to power were certain they had won enough members over to their point of view. When it came to the vote, Verne cast his for the wrong side, and the motion was lost.

No-one ever did find out whether Verne had voted against them on purpose. Some say he had spent most of the debate asleep and, on being suddenly woken, had pressed the wrong voting button in a somnolent daze. The more wicked observers say he had never learnt to read and therefore was unable to decipher the words 'for' and 'against' printed above the voting buttons. But whatever the reason, his foolishness caused inflamed tempers to rupture and a fight broke out, during which Verne was so badly hurt that he was forced to regenerate to save his life. Unfortunately the regeneration process was not as kind as it had been before. What emerged was a very plain face which housed a voice a full octave higher than is normal for a male Time Lord. And such was its sing-song quality it caused those around him to involuntarily snigger when he spoke.

To be laughed at is never fun. To Verne, who had received nothing but praise and admiration since his last regeneration, it was unbearable. And such was his pain that he forced himself to immediately regenerate once more. Alas, the strain on his system was too much. What emerged was a bent, twisted, deformed old man.

Verne was devastated. He regenerated yet again, this time into an amorphous blob that belched and gurgled. He attempted to regenerate one more time, but the hideous monster that emerged was ordered destroyed by the then Lord President.

Although this fate did not await the Doctor, his regeneration could have gone better. Whereas his features had matured slightly and his waist thickened a little, his overall appearance was quite presentable.

It was his mind that was unstable.

Watched by Peri, his American companion, the Doctor slowly climbed to his feet. The poor woman was terrified. Being stuck in space in a time-machine she could not fly along with a human chameleon, did not reassure her at all. Slowly she backed across the console room of the TARDIS, even though she had no idea where she was going or what she could do.

As she reached the door leading to the corridor the Doctor turned to face her. 'Well,' he said enthusiastically. 'What do you think?'

Peri gazed back at the Doctor. 'Er... Er... Er...' Her mouth worked up and down like a demented goldfish. She seemed unable to shape her lips to form words.

'Well?' insisted the Doctor.

'It's . . .' Peri willed herself to speak. 'It's . . . *terrible*!'

The Doctor looked down at his clothes, completely misunderstanding what she had meant. Because he had grown in bulk, the seams of his jacket had split, making him look like some dishevelled tramp. 'Oh, never mind about the clothes,' he said dismissively, 'they're soon changed. What about me – the way I look?'

Peri didn't care how he *looked*. She wanted to know how he had *changed*. Because from where she came people didn't behave as the Doctor had. No-one!

Why doesn't he understand me? Why doesn't he realise how terrified I am. Why hasn't he told me he was capable of such metamorphosis?

These questions remained unanswered largely because Peri hadn't said them out loud. Even if she had the Doctor would not have heard. He was too intent on examining his new face in a mirror. He seemed pleased with it, feeling each feature with the tips of his fingers, like an osteopath gently manipulating a damaged bone.

Satisfied with his new psysiognomy, he pushed past Peri and entered the corridor. Now he required new clothes, garments that would complement his regenerated appearance.

He bounded down the corridor, cautiously followed by Peri. 'You know,' said the Doctor, 'I was never happy with my last incarnation.'

'Whyever not?'

The Doctor paused outside the door of a room. Beyond was a vast store of clothes he had accumulated over the decades. 'He had a feckless charm,' continued the Doctor, 'that wasn't me.'

'That's absolute rubbish.' Peri was indignant. 'You were almost young. I really liked you. You were sweet.'

The Doctor snarled. 'Sweet!' He threw open the door of the wardrobe and blustered in. 'That says it all! Sweet... effete, you mean!'

Peri remained in the corridor for a moment. She was fuming. Her major concern now was how she would cope with such an ogre as the new Doctor.

Suddenly there was a cry from the room. It was one of pain and distress, but not that of a mature man, more the sort of indignant rage uttered by a child when it learns the ground is a painful thing to fall on.

Cautiously, Peri peered around the jamb of the door. Huddled in the middle of the room in a foetal position was the Time Lord, wailing in a low, mournful tone: 'Help me. Help me.'

Peri crossed to the Doctor and bent down at his side. The Time Lord's face looked old and tired. His eyes were lifeless and empty. 'I'm sorry, Peri.' The voice sounded exhausted. 'I've been inconsiderate. You must be terrified by what's happened.'

Although appearing to be in enormous pain, the Doctor continued to reassure her that things weren't as bad as they seemed and that he would soon recover. He also tried to explain what had happened to him, but his use of complicated technical terms made it difficult for her to follow or understand.

The Doctor burbled on, talking about many things almost as though he needed simply to chatter. Most of the time he made sense, but occasionally he slipped into gibberish. Peri felt completely helpless. Although the face before her was that of a stranger she could sense that the *old* Doctor, a man she had grown to love and respect, was, in many ways, still alive.

Peri recalled what had taken place on Androzani Minor, the planet where the Doctor's regeneration had started. How they had both been infected with Spectrox Toxemia and how the Doctor had risked his life to get the antidote, only to find there was enough for one person. This he had given to her without a second thought, then been forced to save his own life by regenerating. All this he had done for her, without pause or hesitation or thought for himself. It seemed that the Doctor would have willingly given up his life, if necessary. Yet, when Peri was called upon to help him, she had panicked, her head filled with thoughts only of her own plight and safety.

Slowly, the Doctor's agitated state receded and he climbed cautiously to his feet. The tattered remains of his coat removed, Peri watched the Time Lord as he inspected a rail of exotic garments. Suddenly she was filled with a feeling of euphoria – *everything would be absolutely fine.*

But then how could she have known of the dangers and trouble still to come?

The empty TARDIS console room was silent but for the gentle purr of the oscillating time rotor. Several lights winked and blinked indicating, for once, the satisfactory running of the time-machine. The room had taken on an air of quiet tranquility.

But this was not to last.

In the corridor outside the shrill voice of Peri was heard. 'You're not serious!'

The door of the console room was thrown open and the Doctor, appearing to have fully recovered, marched in followed by Peri.

The reason for the sudden outburst was the Doctor's choice of clothes. Now it can be said that the Doctor's taste had never been haute couture, but the jacket and trousers which he had decided suited his new persona should have warned Peri of something – they were the choice of a maladjusted personality.

The jacket was long and not dissimilar in design to that worn by an Edwardian paterfamilius. That bit was fine. The main problem was that each panel of the coat was quite different in texture, design and colour. This wouldn't have mattered quite so much if the colours had blended, but they seemed to be cruelly, harshly, viciously at odds with each other. In fact, the coat was so gawdy it would have looked out of place on the back of a circus clown.

But that was only the beginning.

Protruding from the bottom of the jacket were a pair of black and yellow striped trousers, the hems of which rested on red spats, which in turn covered the tops of green shoes. The whole ensemble was finished off with a waistcoast which looked as though someone had been sick on. (For all Peri knew, someone had.) The final touch was a livid green watch chain that at some time must have been stolen from a public lavatory.

Peri continued to remonstrate with the Doctor, urging him to reconsider his clothes. At first he was simply dismissive, but then, for no apparent reason, his mood changed.

'Your name – Peri . . .' The word came out as though the Doctor had a nasty taste in his mouth. 'How did you get a name like that?'

Peri was scared. The Doctor's tone verged on being brutal. 'Well?' he insisted.

'It's a diminutive of my proper name,' she stuttered. 'Perpugilliam.'

The Doctor smirked. 'Do you know what a Peri is?'

She shook her head.

'Of course not! Even if you did you wouldn't admit it... Would you?' The Doctor had started to shout. Peri was petrified. She couldn't make sense of what he was saying.

'As you won't tell me, I shall tell you. A Peri is a good and beautiful fairy in Persian mythology... The interesting thing is... before it became good, it was *evil*!' The Doctor snarled like some caricature mad professor. But Peri wasn't watching this performance in a theatre. This was real. There wasn't any way she could get out of the situation by simply covering her eyes and waiting for the scene to be over.

The Doctor started to move towards her. 'You are thoroughly evil,' he ranted.

'Please, Doctor. This is no longer a joke.'

Peri backed away. As she did, she noticed perched on the console the abandoned mirror the Doctor had used earlier to examine his new face. *A weapon!* she thought. Slowly Peri edged towards it, the Doctor following.

Peri couldn't make any sense of what was happening. Within an hour the Doctor had not only changed into another person, but had gone through fits of agonising pain, sunk to the depths of despair and was now threatening her. *What else could happen?* she thought.

As Peri edged along the console, she suddenly reached to grab the mirror, but the Doctor, now realising her intention, anticipated the move perfectly and savagely lashed out. Peri was lucky and managed to side step the attack. As she did, she snatched up the mirror, but not before the Doctor had leapt at her again, this time making contact. Winded, Peri crashed to the floor, the mirror falling from her grasp. Instantly, like a wild, snarling animal, the Doctor was on top of her.

Peri screamed and thrashed about, praying one of her blows would make contact, but the Doctor was too strong for her. Slowly, deliberately he brought his hands to embrace her throat. On contact he drove his powerful thumbs into her windpipe and pressed firmly. Any hope that this was all a sick, hateful joke departed from her mind. The Doctor *was* going to kill her.

Now knowing she had only seconds to live, Peri felt wildly for the dropped mirror. As she did, she caught a glimpse of her attacker's face – the sight terrified her even more. The Doctor's expression was that of pleasure. He was actually having fun wasting her life.

Choking and coughing, Peri continued her frantic search. Her mouth had now involuntarily dropped open and her protruding tongue jerked backwards and forwards as though attempting to pump air down her restricted windpipe.

Suddenly her hand found the mirror and without pausing she immediately picked it up and started to smash it on the floor. *I have to break it! I must have a sharp edge! I have to be able to hurt him*, she screamed inside her head.

With all her strength she repeatedly struck the mirror on the floor, but it stubbornly refused to break. Peri felt consciousness slipping away from her. She knew that if she blacked out she was dead. With a last enormous effort, she beat and pounded the mirror, but it still wouldn't shatter.

Peri was now consumed by panic and terror. She felt that she was about to slip into the bottomless pit of death and oblivion. Almost as though she were waving herself goodbye, her limbs started to jerk in spasms. A moment later she went limp.

The Doctor, now believing he had killed his victim, loosened his grip slightly. As he did, a terrible leer crossed his face and he started to lick his lips like a glutton who has just had a feast placed before him.

At the same moment, Peri half-opened an eye and saw the hateful delight on the Doctor's face. Summoning up the last shreds of her strength and energy, she held up the mirror so that the Time Lord could see his own expression.

The Doctor froze as he caught sight of his own gruesome image. Then as though he had been savagely slapped across the face he let out a terrible scream at the same moment flinging himself away from Peri and the image in the mirror. On hands and knees, like a frantic, scared baby, the Time Lord quickly crawled across the room, wailing and howling as he went.

Peri lifted herself up onto one elbow, spluttering and coughing. Once her lungs were fully ventilated she started to cry, as much at the pleasure of being alive as with the fear and anger of the assault that had just taken place. She watched the Doctor, as he reached the corner of the room, draw his knees up under his chin and then embrace his own legs. His eyes were like saucers – wild and staring. He was now silent. Then slowly, gently he started to rock backwards and forwards, backwards and forwards, as though desperate to comfort himself.

Peri wondered how long he'd remain that way, and, more desperately, what he would do when he came out of his trance-like state.

3

Enter Professor Edgeworth

Romulus and Remus sat before their respective computer terminals. On the screens before them were a maze of numbers, symbols and calculations. The children had been at play.

Outside it was raining, cold and unfriendly. Outside it was dark. If the twins had looked from their window they would have seen a wet, shabby ginger tom being rather possessive about a few badly-kept flower beds and an area of weed-ridden grass. At least that is what they thought they would have seen. But they would have been wrong. For in the cat's mind, he was fat, virile and sexy. The flower beds were his territory and he was very proud and very defensive of them.

Inside, in the warm, was the twins' world. They didn't know the cat existed. If they had, they would have paid him little attention. For in *their* minds they thought they knew everything about everything, and there was nothing a cat could teach them.

They, of course were wrong, for they didn't realise the cat could teach them survival. The ginger tom could quite easily enter their warm, comfortable world, survive, even have prospered. But the twins couldn't enter his. They would have died of hunger and exposure in a very short period of time. The cat knew this, he knew what the two geniuses didn't know. He also knew it was impossible to calculate the square root of minus three and that Professor Archie Sylvest had made a mistake. It didn't bother him and he wouldn't tell anyone. He had more important things to do – he had his flower beds to guard.

When the whole history of Earth is finally written, it will be shown that cats were the most intelligent creatures ever to have inhabited the planet. The fact they allowed human beings to run things for a while shows their tolerance. They knew the humans would cause havoc and fail, but the cats also knew they would be able to repair everything and make it right again.

In the middle of his favourite flower bed, the ginger tom looked up into the night sky. A thousand miles above his head was a space freighter that had even more secrets than him. To the man-made tracking devices of Earth the freighter was invisibile, as it was protected by a deflector screen. The cat also knew this in the same way he knew that someone from the freighter was being transported to Earth using a matter convertor. The cat smiled. Soon the twins would know what he did, but they would never know that he knew it first!

In the cosiness of their bedroom, Romulus and Remus studied the screens of their computers. They were delighted with what they saw. Their calculations were perfect. What had started as a game had turned into a creation of pure genius.

The twins exchanged a glance of pleasure. They didn't need to say anything as they were aware how each other felt.

It was in this air of self-satisfied pleasure that an elderly man with a shiny bald pate materialised in the middle of the room. He wore a long brown smock and looked a bit like Father Christmas without a beard.

Amazed, the twins watched as the newly-formed imaged settled and became solid.

The old man smiled benevolently, but his sharp, alert eyes were quick to notice the computer screens. 'My name is Edgeworth, Professor Edgeworth,' he said, studying the screens and then nodding with approval and delight at what he saw. He even let out a fruity 'ho-ho-ho' to complement his near Father Christmas image.

'Brilliant!' he said, turning to the twins. 'Absolutely brilliant... A symphony of higher mathematics... I can only be in the company of Romulus and Remus Sylvest.'

'You are. And although you have told us your name, we still do not know who you are and what you are doing here.'

Professor Edgeworth chuckled. He realised he was slightly over-playing the Father Christmas image. 'I've come to pay my respects to your father. A man of great distinction...'

The twins exchanged a nervous glance. 'At this time of night?' Remus' voice was slightly shrill.

'Yes, I must apologise for the lateness of the hour, but I've come a long way.' The words sounded hollow and Edgeworth knew it. He also knew he had to act quickly. It had been his idea to transport down from the freighter alone. He had wanted to avoid the excessive violence he knew a certain crew member of his crew so much enjoyed. But should he fail to take the twins back with him, he would be in a great deal of trouble.

'Look,' he said jovially, 'it seems I've come at a difficult time. Tell your father I will call on him again.'

Professor Edgeworth extended his hand towards Romulus who stared at it for a moment. 'Goodbye, my boy. It's been a pleasure and a privilege.'

Cautiously, Romulus took the proffered hand and shook it. As he did, a fine needle shot out from a ring Edgeworth was wearing and painlessly penetrated the palm of the boy's hand.

Edgeworth turned to the other twin and shook his hand. 'Goodbye, Remus.'

And again the needle did its work.

At first, nothing seemed to happen, then suddenly the twins' expressions went quite blank as though their personalities had been drained from them. Edgeworth ordered the twins to show him their hands. This they did in a passive, unquestioning way. He then asked them where they were, and as hard as they tried, they couldn't remember.

Edgeworth smiled. The drug had worked perfectly. The twins were without conscious memory. When he got them back to the freighter, he would loosen the drug's control, but until then, it was safer that they remained zombie-like.

Edgeworth pulled back the sleeve of his smock and exposed a bracelet. He fiddled with it for a second then ordered the twins to grip his hands. This they did, and a second later the trio dematerialised, leaving a fine powdery deposit on the bedroom floor.

Outside, the ginger tom stood guard over his territory. He knew what had happened. He had sensed the freighter pull out of orbit and set a course for one of the bleakest areas in the universe. He knew all this, but would tell no-one.

The front door of twenty-five Lydall Street was closed with a loud slam. Standing in the hall was Professor Archie Sylvest. He was very drunk. The Voxnic had flowed like a cascading waterfall, but it had not been in the company of computer programmer Vestal Smith. It had been with a less satisfying companion – her husband.

In an attempt to placate him, Archie had persuaded Mr Smith to accompany him to his favourite Voxnic bar and discuss the reasons why he desired so much deep understanding from his wife. It had required what seemed like a lake of Voxnic to convince him that his relationship was platonic, innocent and perfectly reasonable. Archie had no idea whether Mr Smith had believed him, but with the additional comfort of a hundred thousand dollar World Federation currency note, the Neanderthal husband of Vestal Smith had seemed happy to stagger off into the night, his dignity and pride supposedly restored.

Archie lurched along the top landing towards his hateful children's bedroom. It made him feel better when he realised that Nimo had yet to return home. At least she wouldn't see him drunk again or be able to ask him why he looked so pale and why the sleeve of his coat was torn.

Swaying slightly, Archie stood before the door of the twin's room. He wasn't certain whether he should go in as he was far from well enough to cope with their antics.

It was at that moment he noticed the smell.

Cautiously he pushed open the bedroom door. He'd

been right. He had smelt zanium. Archie entered the room and called for his children. There was no reply. He then checked their beds – they were empty and unslept in.

Archie began to panic. He bent down and, like an Indian tracker, picked up a little zanium on the tips of his fingers and sniffed it. Any doubt as to what had happened faded from his mind. Zanium was caused by only one thing: the function of a matter transporter. When a solid body dematerialises, tiny trace elements in the atmosphere called nistron carbonise and fall like very fine, grey snow.

The Voxnic-fuddled mind of Archie began to clear. *How had the intruders got in?* he thought. The house was protected.

Archie staggered out of the bedroom and half-fell, half-stumbled down the stairs and into the sitting room. Standing like some ornament in a scrap yard was the babysitter android – it had been deactivated, something the manufacturers had maintained was impossible.

He then staggered along to the cellar. As with the android, the house protection unit had also been deactivated.

Sylvest sat on the steps of the cellar. In Archie's mind there was no doubt that the twins had been kidnapped. And such was the planning, effort and technology required, he was also convinced it was the work of an alien force. He would have to inform the authorities. Whereas the emotional ties with his hateful children were fragile, there were other considerations to bear in mind. He might not mourne their death, but he might live to regret their work on some scheme inspired by evil for he was convinced they had been kidnapped to this end.

Slowly he shuffled to the nearest transmitter unit. A moment later he was talking to the head of the Intergalactic Task Force.

In the console room aboard the TARDIS, things were again quiet. The Doctor stared at a dial on the control board in front of him. He wasn't certain why he was doing this, as he was none too certain what the dial was telling him. The one thing that was clear to him was that something unpleasant had occurred. The look of hate and mistrust on Peri's face told the whole universe that simple fact.

The Time Lord smiled weakly at his companion. He was desperate for a response, some crumb of information that might help him remember what had occurred. For all that was in his mind was a void, a black impenetrable void. So the Doctor did the obvious thing: he asked.

Peri's response was like a dam bursting. At first he couldn't believe what he was being told, but the passion, feeling and fear of the telling soon changed his mind.

The words continued to pour from Peri's mouth until the Doctor could stand it no longer. But it was too late. He could no longer hide behind his ignorance. The black, protective void that had shielded his mind had been ripped away, like a band aid covering a particularly nasty sore. He now remembered everything and he hated himself for it.

The Doctor clamped his hands to the side of his head and screamed and screamed and screamed. Peri thought the Doctor was having another fit and picked up the mirror in case he again became violent. But instead he turned on the console and started to set switches, twist knobs and pull levers. A new fear entered Peri's head. She wondered if the Doctor still knew how to operate the time-machine. Worse still, she remembered that the Doctor had once said the TARDIS had a self-destruct device and feared he might operate it by mistake.

'Please be careful.'

'Careful? Careful! I tried to kill you! I am a living peril!' Each sentence built in volume until he was shouting, his voice thick with emotion. 'I do not know how to ask your forgiveness,' he wailed.

'You're forgiven, Doc. Just don't destroy the TARDIS by mistake.'

The Doctor was no longer listening. Once more he was at work, this time making fine adjustments to the co-ordinates he had set. 'The universe is at risk with me in this state,' he muttered. 'I must cleanse my mind . . .' He paused dramatically, like a Victorian actor. Peri braced herself, ready for anything. 'Self-abnegation,' was the cry from the Doctor. He looked around, as though waiting for a burst of applause from the stalls. 'Self-abnegation in some hellish wilderness!' Each word rolled and thundered around the console room. 'Ten days – ten years – a thousand! Of what account is time to me?'

Poor Peri gave up. She couldn't keep pace with the Doctor's changing mood. She now wished he had killed her. At least that would have been quick. 'A thousand years?' she enquired. 'Aren't you forgetting? I'm from Earth. Our allotted span is about seventy years, and I've already had twenty of them.'

The Doctor looked haughtily at his companion. 'I

was speaking figuratively. It shouldn't come to that.'

'Look, Doc, I really do forgive you. I now understand what you're going through. You're not in control of yourself. All you need is rest. A short holiday.'

'I need a hermitage.' He hadn't heard a word Peri had said. 'Some utterly comfortless place where we can suffer together.'

'Hang on.' For Peri this wasn't good news. 'Why should *I* be made to suffer. It was *you* who tried to kill *me*. I am the innocent party here.'

'Who in this life is ever purely innocent?' The Victorian actor had gone. In his place was an old Testament prophet, determined to see no-one have a good time. The Doctor's voice had also dropped a full octave for this role. If it hadn't been so frightening, Peri would have found it all rather impressive.

'You have been chosen,' the Doctor boomed, jabbing a rigid index finger at Peri, 'to minister to my needs . . . They will be very simple . . . But *nothing* must be allowed to interfere with my period of contemplation.'

'This isn't fair!' Peri was now on the verge of tears. 'And *who* is supposed to have appointed me your servant?'

'Providence!'

'Look, Doctor, you're in a crazy state of mind. If you want to go anywhere, go to your home planet. They can help you there.' Then even more desperately she added, 'I don't think you realise how mentally unstuck you've become.'

'I have already spoken!'

'Then if you want somewhere really desolate, I suggest you try the Bronx or downtown New York.

Because while you're enjoying a thousand years of desolation, at least I'll be able to get a train home!'

The Doctor didn't hear the sarcasm. Already he seemed to have entered a trance-like state. 'I have decided on my place of hermitage,' he mutterd. 'It is in the far corner of the Baxus Major galaxy.'

As he spoke he struck the main control on the console and the TARDIS started to lurch and judder towards its destination.

Such was the unexpected movement, Peri was thrown to the floor. 'Why are you doing this?' she screamed. 'Where are you taking me?' The Doctor gazed down at the prostrate Earth woman, indifferent to her confusion and anguish.

'We, my child, are going to Titan Three . . . That is where I shall repent . . . In the most desolate place in the universe.'

Peri buried her head in her hands and silently wept. She could only hope the Doctor would have a period of rationality. When he did, she would demand to be taken back to Earth. As far as she was concerned, he could travel the universe alone pretending to be whoever or whatever he wanted. But she no longer wanted to stay and be his terrified audience.

But until the Doctor did take a turn for the better, all she could do was wait . . . And it was the waiting that terrified Peri most of all.

4

Mestor the Magnificent

A shabby balk carrier ploughed its way slowly through the empty wastes of space. At first sight there seemed nothing special about the ship. Perhaps it was a little shabbier than the majority of commercial freighters which travelled the space lanes to Baxus Major. It was possible, if you were familiar with the XV class of balk carriers, that you might have queried an irregular line of holes along one side of its hull. But then, on the other hand, you might have dismissed it as meteorite damage. After all, the freighter did look very neglected, as though no-one really cared.

And that was what you were supposed to think. For the reality was that balk carrier XV 773 was a highly efficient battle cruiser.

Seated on the bridge of the ship was Professor Edgeworth. He now looked tired and drawn, his Father Christmas joviality gone. For a moment he sat watching the flickering lights of the flight computer. Even as a child, Edgeworth had found comfort in watching flashing lights. At times he wished he were a child again.

Professor Bernard Edgeworth didn't really exist as a

person. The name was real as was the man who used it, but the person who used it also told lies. Edgeworth's real name was Azmael, and, like the Doctor, was a renegade Time Lord who had tired of life on Gallifrey and decided to make his fortune elsewhere. But unlike the Doctor, the High Council had not so readily accepted Azmael's departure. He was far too knowledgeable and important to be allowed to wander freely about the universe. Too many enemies were waiting to steal his skill, experience and knowledge.

So the High Council had decided to kill him. That was their first mistake.

Of course, they had the order of execution dressed up. In his absence he had been found guilty of all sorts of invented crimes, the evidence against him being about as credible as the integrity of the paid witnesses who presented it.

So, for the first and last time in the history of Gallifrey an execution squad had been despatched. It hadn't proved difficult to find Azmael as he wasn't really hiding. He just wanted to be left in peace. But the second mistake the High Council had made was the choice of assassins – Seedle warriors.

There is no such thing as a pleasant Seedle warrior. They are all brutal psychopaths who take enormous pleasure in killing. Azmael's execution squad was no exception. Arriving on Vitrol Minor, where Azmael was living, the so-called warriors set about eliminating the populace, justifying the genocide as the elimination of witnesses to the destruction of a Time Lord. For the warriors, it was like being on holiday. They had three days of glorious, blood-drenched fun. It wasn't until the fourth day that they noticed their real quarry had escaped.

Azmael immediately returned to Gallifrey and started proceedings to indict the Lord President and High Council. Being professional politicians, they believed they could survive any accusation made by him, but they had too easily forgotten the atrocity committed. On Gallifrey there is only one inviolate law – Time Lords are forbidden to directly interfere with life forms on other planets. With the entire population of Vitrol Minor slaughtered, the High Council would require massive bribes to buy their innocence.

But buy it they did.

Slowly evidence came to light showing that Azmael had himself employed the Seedle warriors to destroy the populace of Vitrol Minor. His motive was supposedly to gain the mineral rights of the planet. The fact there wasn't a useful gram of any known mineral to be found on the planet seemed to disturb no-one.

Except Azmael, of course.

He was very angry. He knew the High Council would wriggle out of the charges. In fact, he was so angry they could escape judgement that he took a laser rifle and gunned them down in their own council chamber.

It saddened Azmael that he had been forced to adopt the ultimate sanction, but at the end of the day it is sometimes the only method to deal with corrupt politicians.

To some people this is known as revolution. To others it must always remain murder. Poor Azmael was so disgusted with what he had been forced to do that he publicly declared himself an outcast and departed from Gallifrey.

The new High Council, who were just as cynical as the old one, but less corrupt, declared Azmael a hero. After all he had done them a favour. They had been waiting many regenerations for their chance of power. He had made it possible. But the first act of the new council was to set up a committee to learn how Azmael had so easily entered the Council Chamber with a laser rifle. Although they had approved of his magnificent cleansing of a corruption, they weren't over-keen that he, or any other fanatic, should succeed so easily again.

After many years of travel, Azmael arrived at a planet called Jaconda. To him it was the most beautiful place he had ever seen. It was green and its handsome birdlike inhabitants enjoyed an easy carefree way of life which he readily adopted. Likewise, the Jacondans accepted him and soon he was their elected President.

But the fairy tale didn't last.

Lurking in the history of Jaconda was a legendary race of gastropods known as Sectoms. These were not the small, aggravating creatures of the domestic garden, but slugs the size of men who were capable of devouring forests, destroying meadows and reducing to desert once fertile land. Not only did they support a massive appetite, but also a brain and cunning equal to any intelligence in the universe.

Where these creatures had come from was a mystery. Why they had come to Jaconda and conquered the planet, only to disappear again, was another conundrum. As the legends and myths grew about the Sectoms, people began to wonder whether they had ever existed.

That was a mistake . . .

One night, not long after Azmael had become President, a terrible thunder storm had occurred. The rain had poured down destroying the harvest, while the lightning, much like a Seedle warrior, had attacked anything that took its fancy.

Deep in an ancient forest, a huge beautiful mustock tree had become one of its victims. In life, the tree had been positioned precariously on the edge of a steep bank and its sudden, violent demise had sent it crashing down the slope in such a way that its thick, stubby branches had ripped open the surface of the ground to reveal hundreds of round leathery objects.

The rain had continued to batter the scarred soil, at the same time washing, caressing, cleansing the rubber shapes. When the rain stopped, the Jacondan sun took over and gently warmed the spheres. A few days later, strange noises could be heard from within the shells. The objects were eggs. And they were about to hatch!

It was some months before Jaconda knew of its fate. One morning it awoke to find an army of gastropods led by a hideous shape calling himself Mestor the Magnificent. Jacondan weapons had proved ineffectual against their slimy targets, so to save life Azmael had ordered his adopted people to surrender.

As though making up for the thousands of years the eggs had lain unnourished in the ground, the gastropods had embarked on a feast so gargantuan that it all but destroyed most of the planet's vegetation. What had been a beautiful, living, green paradise was reduced to a scorched lifeless rock. It was now a matter of time before everyone, including the gastropods, died of starvation!

Azmael turned away from the computer lights – they no longer pleased him. Neither did the fact that he was the slave of Mestor. The expediency of bowing to his will was one thing, but the thought of spending the rest of his days satisfying the needs of a psychotic wind-bag was more than he could bear.

Azmael's thoughts were interrupted by the scuff of a

boot against the metal deck of the ship. It was Noma. 'The twins have been secured,' he said.

The Time Lord nodded, then watched as the Jacondan made his way to the ship's galley. Azmael had never trusted Noma, not even before the Sectoms had arrived. He was too sly and often wore a smile that verged on a leer. Now that he was a captain in Mestor's special squad, he couldn't be trusted at all.

On the other hand, Drak, his lieutenant, was quite different. On a security monitor Azmael could see him tucking the twins into their bunks. The domesticity of the scene was almost incongruous aboard a warship, especially as Drak was taking such an obvious fatherly pleasure from his task.

Azmael flicked a switch and the screen went blank. He was too tough and too old to be unduly affected by sentiment, but the feelings he had experienced on Gallifrey, just prior to 'executing' the High Council, were beginning to stir again.

Mestor must die, he thought. *Whatever the cost!*

What's more, Azmael knew he would have to kill him soon.

As soon as Drak had left the room, Romulus and Remus climbed out of bed. The drug they had been given to restore parts of their memory had worked rapidly. They were still confused and a little disorientated, but one thing was clear – they were prisoners aboard a space ship and they weren't at all pleased about it.

The twins speculated as to how soon their absence from Earth would be noticed and what their drunken father and academically spaced-out mother would do about it.

Romulus cursed the fecklessness of his parents, while Remus was a little more practical. Quickly, his nimble fingers unclipped a wall panel to reveal a mass of wires and printed circuits. Desperately trying to remember the intergalactic colour code, he started to disconnect several of the cables from a junction box.

'What are you doing?' asked Romulus.

'Trying to rig some sort of distress call.'

Romulus scoffed, highly suspicious as to whether anyone would hear, even if his brother proved successful.

Undeterred, though, Remus worked on.

It had taken the Intergalactic Task Force thirty seconds to scramble a squadron of star fighters. It had taken them even less time to locate Azmael's freighter. Whether through tiredness, or a subconscious desire to be followed, Azmael had inadvertently switched off the deflector shield and his ship had become visible to the tracking stations on Earth.

At the head of the 'V' formation of star fighters was Lieutenant Hugo Lang. He was a tall, slim, good-looking man in his mid-twenties. He had graduated top of his year from Star Fighter pilot school and it was believed he was destined for great things. In fact, Hugo was every inch a hero in the making, and all it now required was combat experience to confirm it, which his present mission would provide. Although his assignment was fairly routine, and therefore quite safe, the kidnapping of the Sylvest twins would generate a lot of publicity. All Hugo had to do was bring them safely back to be declared a hero. At least, that is what those who were stage-managing his career thought. Unfortunately they didn't know they were sending an inexperienced pilot up against one of the most ruthless leaders in the universe. Mestor may have somewhat theatrically billed himself as 'The Magnificent', but it would have been more accurate if he had called himself 'The Merciless'.

As the squadron made visual contact, the onboard computers automatically started to scan the freighter, transmitting the information back to Control on Earth for analysis.

Everything seemed to be going well. All that Hugo had to do now was challenge the freighter and order it to return to Earth. If its captain refused, then he was allowed, under intergalactic law, to open fire and disable the ship. The freighter would then be towed back to Earth.

At least, that was the theory.

As the squadron took up its attack formation, Hugo's radio started to crackle with an urgent message from Intergalactic Control. It stated he was about to arrest a freighter that had been lost, believed destroyed, eight months earlier.

Momentarily confused, Hugo peered out of his cockpit and read off the registration number emblazoned on the side of the ship's hull – XV 733. Confirmation was immediate – it was the lost freighter. Hugo smiled. Not only would he become a hero, but he would also pick up a fat salvage fee.

As he calculated how he might spend his new-found wealth, an irregular pulsing broke in on his headphone. Quickly the noise settled down and become an intergalactic distress call. Remus's fiddling had worked, but, alas, too late. A moment later the freighter went into warp drive and disappeared down a crack in time. Unless Hugo acted quickly, his chance of promotion and wealth would follow a similar descending spiral to the bottom of no-where.

To become the sort of hero Hugo desired to be isn't a difficult thing. It doesn't require great intelligence or courage, wit or humour, or any of the other attributes prized so much by human beings. Hugo's sort of heroism, that is political heroism, simply requires two things: to be in the right place at the right time; and for the act to receive public approbation, backed, of course, by those holding social and political authority. Sometimes, especially if the act of heroism is particularly stupid, it helps if the perpetuator dies. True heroism, like saving someone from a burning space shuttle, requires enormous courage, presence of mind and compassion for your own species, especially if you don't know the person you're saving. True heroism cannot be overpraised. Political heroism is a shabby imitation of the real thing and is best left to those with shabby, mediocre ambitions.

Hugo Lang, starfighter pilot, was not only politically motivated, but was also greedy for salvage money. He was also aware that if both fame and fortune were not to allude him, his next move had to be a bold one. It also had to be the right one.

Rapidly, Hugo barked orders into his radio, then flicked an override switch on his control column. A moment later, followed by his squadron, he disappeared down the same hole in time the freighter had taken.

Perhaps it was his lack of experience, or simply his desire for success, but no-one at Intergalactic Control could understand why the obvious had not occurred to

Hugo – the XV class of freighter was incapable of warp drive.

Azmael paced up and down the bridge of his ship annoyed with his own stupidity. It had been his intention to take the twins to a safe house on Titan Three where he would be able to fulfill his plan. Now he was being pursued by six starfighters, with little chance of escape. To engage them in battle would be suicide. Even though the heavy armaments of his craft could outgun most ships in the universe, a concentrated attack of six starfighters would prove too much for the freighter's defensive force shield.

Angrily, Azmael slapped the console in front of him. It had taken him weeks to convince Mestor of the viability of his plan. Even if the freighter could destroy the fighters, Mestor wouldn't allow him to stay at the safe house.

Rapidly, the Time Lord pressed a series of buttons on the flight computer and the freighter, shuddering slightly as the warp engines were disengaged, slowed to sub-light speed.

Ahead lay Titan Three.

Once more Azmael manipulated the controls and the freighter slipped into orbit around the tiny planet. With a little luck, the Time Lord reasoned, he might be able to use its mass to play hide and seek, thereby giving him the chance to pick the fighters off one at a time.

Hugo Lang thought otherwise. As his squadron emerged from warp drive, their tracking instruments immediately pinpointed Azmael's ship as it slipped over the horizon of the planet before him. Confidently,

Hugo spoke into his radio and the starfighters manoeuvred effortlessly into battle formation.

As the squadron sped towards Titan Three, the flight divided, half skirting the eastern rim of the planet, while the remainder, led by Hugo, turned westward. Seconds later the pincer movement was complete and the hapless freighter trapped. Azmael responded with a half-hearted flight of missiles which the starfighters easily avoided.

As Hugo was about to give his final instructions for their attack, his ship started to pitch and toss as though caught in a pocket of turbulence. Hugo checked his flight computer, but the instrument was unable to provide an answer.

One by one, the other starfighters reported similar problems, so Hugo ordered the squadron to withdraw while they reconsidered the situation.

If Hugo Lang had been a more experienced pilot, possibly less arrogant, and certainly less concerned with his own glory, he would have realised much sooner that the further his squadron distanced itself from the freighter, the worse the turbulence grew. So, instead of pondering on the more immediate problem, Hugo spent the last few seconds of his squadron's existence asking his flight computer questions it couldn't answer. He was still shouting at the confused machine when the cause of the turbulence appeared over the rim of the planet.

At first sight, it was not unlike a massive aurora borealis, except that the whirling mists of colour were contained in a blue haze that undulated like a balletic amoeba. For a moment, the phenomenon seemed to hover, as though studying the starfighters. Hugo gazed back, as much impressed by its beauty as confused why the mass still didn't register on his ship's sensors. Even at this late stage, Hugo did not realise the enormous danger he faced.

Suddenly a finger of blue mist shot towards the nearest fighter and, on contact, the ship vaporised.

'Scramble!' Hugo screamed into his radio.

Instantly the squadron broke formation and built up speed ready to enter warp drive. As they did, a massive blue fist emerged from the main body of the cloud and enveloped three of the fighters. They, too, vaporised.

Realising they couldn't outrun the cloud, the two remaining fighters turned in a steep arc and, with laser cannons firing, flew at battle speed towards the swirl of colour. For good measure, Hugo also fired a full broadside of missiles, but all to little effect. The cloud simply absorbed the energy with an almost graceful ease.

Undeterred, the fighters flew on, this time firing Baston torpedoes. Under normal circumstances, one torpedo would have been sufficient to destroy a small moon. Two, a planet the size of Earth. Yet the cloud took four without seeming to disturb an atom of its structure.

As the fighters drew nearer to the mist, Hugo could see a small black irregular shape at its heart. Sensing this was some sort of control centre, he lined up his laser cannons and fired, scoring a direct hit.

Suddenly the soft, Turneresque colouring of the cloud turned harsh and livid. Hugo gave a small, boyish cheer, but his celebration was short lived. Instead of its destruction, the cloud launched a ball of blue fire which rapidly moved towards the second fighter. Although the pilot took evasive action, twisting, diving, wriggling everyway possible, the ball found its target with ease and the burning fighter silently exploded in the vacuum of space.

Again, the cloud launched another fireball. Determined not to meet the same fate as his command, Hugo thrust his craft into a massive power drive towards Titan Three. His intention was to pull out of vertical descent just before hitting its atmosphere. With luck, the following fireball would be travelling too fast to do the same and would enter the atmosphere and disintegrate.

But it wasn't to be.

Such was the speed and force of the dive, plus the gravitational pull of the planet, that Hugo was unable to correct his descent in time, and the ship hit the thin atmosphere with a sickening thud. Although the ship remained in one piece, there was little its pilot could do to correct its rapid fall. In a last desperate attempt, Hugo fired the main retro rockets, but the fighter continued to plummet towards the surface of the planet.

Aboard the freighter, Azmael watched in amazement. Although impressed by the cloud's performance, he was more than a little concerned as to whether it would prove as hostile towards him.

Azmael lowered himself into the pilot's chair and slipped on the safety harness. Like the crew of the starfighters, he wasn't going to give up without a fight.

As he snapped the fastener of the harness shut, the bridge suddenly filled with a misty red light which then wrapped itself around the trapped Time Lord. At the same moment, his head was filled with a slurping, sibilant voice he knew only too well – Mestor's!

Deliberately, angrily, hatefully, the voice began to slash at Azmael's tired mind, damning the Time Lord for his incompetence, for endangering the mission and for causing him to waste so much energy and effort.

Mestor continued his mental attack until the Time Lord thought his mind would explode. Then as suddenly as it had started, the assault stopped and the red mist evaporated. At the same moment, the cloud which had destroyed the starfighters also dissolved.

Azmael collapsed back into his chair, his body rigid and his mind raw. As the pain eased, he slowly opened his eyes and saw the sneering face of Noma. 'You never did understand the Lord Mestor's power,' he said. 'He's everywhere. Can do anything.'

Azmael was reluctant to concede that Mestor had the power of a deity, but he could not deny he had destroyed six fighters with little apparent effort. It also made him wonder how regularly Mestor monitored his thoughts and how much he knew of his plans to destroy the hateful gastropod.

Azmael watched as Noma operated the controls of the ship – he was preparing to land. It seemed that the Time Lord would be allowed to continue his work on Titan Three. This surprised him. Perhaps Mestor wasn't as all-seeing as Noma thought.

It didn't occur to Azmael that Mestor knew precisely what he was up to and didn't care. He didn't need to. He had the power to kill the Time Lord any time, any place, he wanted.

5

Titan Three

It is strange how coincidence can seem to conspire. Titan Three has the reputation of being the most desolate and unvisited planet in the universe. Yet all of a sudden, disparate events had caused several parties to arrive more or less simultaneously.

First had been the Doctor and his highly distraught companion, Peri.

Nearby, and as yet unknown to the Doctor, Azmael's ship was making a controlled landing.

Closer still was Hugo Lang. His ship was far from controlled. But the firing of the retro rockets had had far more effect than he had dared hoped for.

On the ground, the Doctor and Peri emerged from the TARDIS and surveyed the bleak horizon. In spite of Peri's gallant attempt to persuade the Doctor to the contrary, he still wanted to be a hermit. Worse still, he had decided that the TARDIS was too comfortable a place to live and that a dank, draughty cave would be much more suitable.

Like a Victorian explorer, his hand shielding his eyes against the dull, watery sun, the Doctor continued to scan the horizon. A cold wind had started to blow, disturbing the powdery, grey dust that covered the surface of the planet. Peri began to cough as she inhaled the dusty air and then started to shiver. The thought of spending the rest of her life in such an unpleasant environment did not please her at all and she felt as though she wanted to cry and cry.

What the Doctor felt at that particular moment was a mystery, even to himself. Although he still maintained his David Livingstone stance, his hand on his forehead like the peak of a cap, his mind, in fact, had gone blank. Even the deafening sound of screaming engines, like those of a starfighter falling out of control, couldn't penetrate the inner sanctum of his conscious mind.

It wasn't until the fighter crashed and exploded that his mind slipped back into gear.

Picking himself up from where he had been blown, the Doctor looked eagerly around. Some distance away he could see a burning wreck and was puzzled as to how it had got there. Peri, who had thrown herself flat on the ground the instant the fighter had appeared, also scrambled to her feet.

Without a word, the Doctor leapt forward towards the wreck. Suddenly he wanted to be a hero. A ship had crashed. Lives were in danger. He must go to the rescue. With mightly bounds, he dashed across the rough terrain with Peri in pursuit.

As they approached the fighter, there was a small explosion sending up a column of flame and black smoke. This seemed to delight and excite the Doctor even more. In his mind this was *real* danger. Peri wished he still wanted to be a hermit.

As they arrived, they saw the body of Hugo lying near the wreck. Fortunately he had been thrown clear before his ship had burst into flames. Quickly the Doctor felt for the young man's pulse. It was still there, weak, but still pumping.

With effortless ease, and much to Peri's amazement, the Doctor scooped up the unconscious pilot and ran back to the TARDIS.

While Peri searched for the medical kit, the Doctor examined Hugo for broken bones. Apart from the odd cut, a little bruising and a few burns, he seemed otherwise undamaged.

As Peri carried the medical kit into the console room, the TARDIS shuddered slightly. The wreckage of the fighter had given up and exploded.

Peri noticed that once more the Doctor's expression had changed and wondered who he thought he was now. Christian Barnard? Pasteur? Alexander Fleming? Madame Curie? Whoever he fancied himself to be, Peri hoped he had stopped being a hero and had forgotten about being a hermit.

As the Doctor dressed Hugo's wounds, the young man started to regain consciousness. 'The children . . .' he muttered, 'my ship . . . my squadron!'

Suddenly Hugo's eyes were wide open. With unexpected speed, he pulled out a small gun from a holster at his waist. Using both hands to steady it, he pointed it at the Doctor. 'Murderer!' he screamed. 'You destroyed my whole command!'

Quickly, the Doctor snatched the gun and simultaneously chopped Hugo across the side of the neck. Instantly the pilot was rendered unconscious.

'He was going to kill me.' The Doctor's voice was squeaky with a mixture of outrage and fear.

'Poor guy... Think what he must have suffered.'

'That is quite beside the point. For all you seem to care, I could be lying dead at your feet this very moment.'

'But you're not. You're safe, *Doc.*' She stressed the word *Doc*, knowing how much he hated the diminutive. 'The point is, can you save *him*?'

The Doctor folded his arms and turned away. Such was his petulance that Peri expected him to mince out of the console room. Instead, he said, 'You never cease to amaze me. You are asking me to revive a man who had every intention of terminating my life.'

'That's right.'

Peri leant forward, tugged at a plastic tag attached to the tunic of Hugo's jacket until it was free and held it up for the Doctor to read: *Lieutenant Hugo Lang, Intergalactic Task Force, 'A' Squadron.*

'Oh...' said the Doctor at last. 'A policeman.'

'That's right. Now get to work and make him well again!'

Reluctantly the Doctor bent down and continued his ministration. The Time Lord was puzzled. He was aware that he was having lapses of memory, but couldn't understand why Peri was being so aggressive. Come to that, he couldn't remember why they had come to Titan Three. Perhaps the two things were linked.

In fact, the more the Doctor thought about the general situation, the more confused he became. Why had Hugo accused him of destroying his squadron? And who were the children he seemed so concerned about? Come to that, what was Hugo doing so far from his home planet? He couldn't imagine that Titan Three was part of his normal beat.

The more the Doctor wondered, the more he realised how confused and muddled his mind was. He would have to do something about it.

But what?

6

An Unsafe Safe House

Titan Three has always been accused of being the bleakest, most miserable planet in the universe. Scenically, it is no bleaker than any other small planet devoid of vegetation. The real problem with Titan is that its thin atmosphere contains a very rare gas nicknamed Titan Melancholia. It isn't at all poisonous, but prolonged inhalation can cause depression in humanoid life forms.

Azmael had discovered Titan Three while searching for somewhere to live after his self-imposed exile from Gallifrey. At that time he very much wanted to be alone and Titan seemed to offer him precisely that.

He had been surprised when he had discovered buildings on the planet. And even more surprised when he had learnt they had been built by people from a nearby solar system that no longer existed.

It wasn't until he discovered a still functioning computer that he learnt of their sad fate.

Originally the buildings had been erected to house a research unit and monitoring base for the solar system, Maston Viva. Before building the centre, all the usual checks and tests had been made, including a close examination of the atmosphere. Although a gas unknown to the Mastons (Titan Melancholia) had been detected, exhaustive research seemed to indicate it was inert and safe to breathe. So the centre was built.

It wasn't until some time later that it was noticed that people who spent more than six months on the planet became strangely depressed. At first this was dismissed as nothing more than an over-reaction to Titan's bleak environment, so the tour of duty was shortened to three months.

This did little to help.

Scientist, technician and labourer alike started to abandon their work in favour of writing long, introverted, painfully self-critical novels and essays. When summoned home, they refused to go, preferring to stay on Titan to complete their self-imposed tasks.

Such was the all pervading gloom of the place that *Mein Kampf* and the works of Strindberg were read as light comic relief.

It was during one of these intense periods of introspection that an enormous burst of radiation wiped out the population of Maston Viva. The scientists, whose function it was to warn of such impending disasters, were mortified. On checking their computers, they found that the radiation cloud had been visible for days, and if they had been more attentive to their duties, the danger could have been neutralised.

Suddenly, the pain of life had overtaken the agony of art. There was little left for the scientists to do. After each of them had completed a long, soul-searching autobiography, they committed mass suicide.

They were the first and last victims of Titan Melancholia. Shortly afterwards, it was discovered that a daily glass of Voxnic acted as the perfect antidote to the side effect of the gas. But such were the terrible events that had taken place on the planet that nobody wanted to live there.

Originally Azmael had earmarked the planet as a bolt-hole in case the High Council of Gallifrey had changed its mind and again sent a squad of Seedle Warriors to kill him.

But that was a long time ago.

Nowadays, Seedle Warriors seemed relatively harmless compared with the paranoid ambition displayed by Mestor.

Yet here he was again, this time watching two immature boys struggle with chalk and blackboard to complete equations that had been set for them.

The twins weren't happy, being unused to such primitive implements. Their fingers were sore from holding the chalk and their arms ached from the effort of scratching their calculations on the squeaky blackboard. Although they had complained bitterly, Azmael had shown little sympathy. 'You've brought this on yourself. If you hadn't rigged that silly distress beacon aboard my ship, I would have let you use the computer . . . Now I can't trust you.'

The twins worked on, but they were running out of patience. The drug which controlled their minds was beginning to weaken, and their stubbornness was returning.

'There's no point to what we're doing,' complained Remus.

'That's right,' echoed Romulus. 'Why don't you tell us what this is about? The equations you've set us could be done by an idiot. You don't need *us* for this sort of work.'

Azmael nodded. Romulus was absolutely right. What they had been given to do was simply to test their co-operation and the accuracy of their work. Mestor had insisted.

'To be honest, I do not know what is intended for you. You must understand that I am also a prisoner. I must do as I am told.'

The twins weren't certain whether to believe him. 'Then tell us who your master is,' they said as one voice.

Cautiously, Azmael looked over his shoulder as though expecting to find Mestor listening. 'His name would mean nothing,' he said quietly. 'But understand that he is a creature of infinite ambition.' Azmael glanced over his shoulder once more. 'He will use anything and anyone to gain his ends.'

'Including us?' said Romulus.

Azmael nodded. 'He requires the gift of your genius.'

'He shan't have it,' said Remus, cutting in. 'We shall fight him if necessary.'

As the boy spoke, a swirl of red light formed into a hologram of the most repulsive creature the twins had ever seen.

It was Mestor.

'Fight me!' his rasping voice boomed. 'Beware, boy . . . So far, I have been prepared to put up with your childish obduracy. But no longer! Fail to obey me and I shall have your minds removed from your bodies and use them as I wish . . . Do you understand?'

Terrified, the twins nodded. As they did, the image of Mestor faded.

'I did try to warn you,' said Azmael. 'Believe what Mestor says. He does not make idle threats.'

*

Lieutenant Hugo Lang lay prostrate on the floor of the TARDIS console room, his wounds dressed, a pillow under his head and a blanket covering his body. He looked cosy and snug, which is more than the Doctor did.

Something was agitating him.

Peri watched, as the restless Time Lord paced up and down like a caged tiger, and feared what he might do next.

'Something's very wrong.' The Doctor's voice had changed slightly, his diction had become more precise. Peri wondered who he thought he was this time. 'As a rule, most deduction is elementary, requiring little more than the application of logic. But to be honest,' he continued, indicating Hugo, 'the current situation has me baffled. Something is very amiss, my dear Peri. I sense evil at work.'

'The lieutenant isn't evil.'

'I'm not talking about him.'

'Then who?'

'The person behind the reason that brought him here.'

Peri was not only becoming confused, but concerned. She didn't want the Doctor to become involved in yet more trouble.

'Can't we just leave?' she said plaintively. 'Whatever may be going on here doesn't concern us.'

'It certainly does.' The Doctor paused in his pacing. 'My very being exists to solve crimes. I have spent a lifetime developing my powers of observation. Married to my unerring sense of logic, I have refined the routine of criminal investigation to that of a science!'

Suddenly Peri knew who the Doctor thought he was: *Sherlock Holmes.* How long, she wondered, would it be before he was racing across the planet looking for Professor Moriarty?

'You must understand my need to get to the bottom of this business.'

How could she? The Doctor wasn't Sherlock Holmes, neither were they in Victorian London.

'Even as a child, my gift was well-developed. With the use of pure logic and observation I deduced where babies came from.'

Peri yawned, hoping it would distract the Doctor from his fantasy. But if he noticed he didn't respond, continuing as though every word was true.

'My mother had always insisted that the stork brought babies, but living in a large city I found that difficult to believe, as the arrival of infants was frequent but the sighting of storks was very rare. In fact, it wasn't until the age of ten that I saw my first stork – and that was in a zoo!'

'So once and for all I decided to solve the mystery. Word had it that a baby was due next door, so I set about watching our neighbour's house. Apart from someone called a mid-wife, no-one else entered or left that dwelling until I heard the cry of a new-born babe.'

'No stork either, huh?'

'Not even a sparrow. Now it had not gone unnoticed by me that the mid-wife had arrived carrying a large satchel. She had no sooner entered the house than I had heard an infant crying. I therefore deduced that the mid-wife had brought the baby in her bag!'

A bemused smile spread across Peri's face. 'Brilliant. A very clever deduction for an unenlightened child . . .' She paused. The look on the Doctor's face told her that she had said the wrong thing.

'So I was wrong on that occasion!' he shouted. 'I

couldn't help it if my idiot parents had refused to tell me the facts of life . . .'

'But if you were mistaken once, you could be again.'

The Doctor had started to sulk. 'Rubbish! I have since perfected my method.'

Peri gave up. What could she say to a man, who in the space of a few hours, had played Jack the Ripper, wanted to be a hermit, and was now basing his personality on a fictional detective? To argue seemed pointless.

She knew it could prove very dangerous, especially as something else had occurred to her which made her feel rather sick.

Up until now the Doctor had played at being rather silly, if not pathetic characters. True, he had tried to kill Peri and in his remorse had taken her to a remote, barren planet, which she had no way of leaving alone. Under more normal circumstances any single one of these acts would be considered outrageous. But this was far from any ordinary situation – the perpetrator was a Time Lord.

It was this fact, until now, that Peri had overlooked. What the Doctor had done was nothing compared to what he was ultimately capable of. All it required was one wrong word at a critical moment and he might convince himself he wanted to dominate the universe. Should that occur, then nothing would be safe. The Doctor's knowledge and ablity to manipulate time made it possible for him to change or destroy everything.

But how was she to prevent it?

As Peri thought about the problem, the Doctor started to pace up and down again. Perhaps the simplest way, she considered, would be to play along with him. If the Doctor wanted to be Sherlock Holmes, she would be his Watson. By acting out his fantasy he might begin to trust her. When the Doctor next tried to swap his personality, she might be able to control or direct him. With a little luck, she might also, gradually, lead him back to his 'real' self – whatever or whoever that should turn out to be.

At least she could try.

'What are you going to do?' asked Peri, tentatively.

'Solve the riddle, of course!' said the Doctor, rummaging in his pocket.

For a moment she thought he was looking for his Meersham.

'Have you seen my jellybabies?'

Peri shook her head.

'It's just that I think much better when I'm chewing.' The Doctor smiled awkwardly. 'Never mind, I'll have to do without them.'

'You still haven't said how you plan to solve the riddle – whatever it is.'

'First, we must consider the facts,' said the Doctor, crossing to Hugo. 'In spite of the fact that our young friend here has been shot down, he still has one other thought in his mind – the children.'

So far, Peri couldn't fault his logic.

'Now, let us assume he is here to find the children, and whoever has them, shoots him and the rest of his squadron down.'

Again, the Doctor's reasoning was sound.

'Therefore, as Hugo crashed on this planet, one of two things could have happened. Number one: he was shot down while pursuing the abductor of the children. Number two: the abductor is based on this planet and destroyed the squadron as it approached.'

The Doctor crossed to the console and switched on the scanner-screen. 'I am inclined to believe that the villain is here on Titan Three.'

'How come?' said Peri, trying hard not to sound too much like the traditional, dumb sidekick of a fictional detective. 'You said yourself there wasn't any life here.'

'There wasn't... But things change.' The Doctor pointed at Hugo. 'He's here. And so are we.'

Peri didn't see the sense of the Time Lord's observation, but bit her tongue, determined not to comment.

'I can see from your expression that you don't agree.'

'Not at all.' She sounded phoney and unconvincing.

'You're right to criticise. What I have just said contradicts my own methods. But when the villain of this particularly nasty piece of work could be anywhere in the universe, it sometimes pays to use one's intuition. Therefore, I suggest we start by checking Titan Three.'

Peri smiled, delighted to hear that the Doctor was once more making sense.

'And there we are!' he shouted excitedly, the index finger of his right hand, ridged and commanding, as it pointed at the screen.

Peri turned to look but could see nothing but the dust covered surface of the planet.

'There!' he shouted. 'That hump!'

Quickly, the Doctor operated the zoom and the area of interest was enlarged.

'Use your eyes,' he commanded. 'Look at that hump's symetry. That's no part of nature's handiwork.'

Peri moved closer to the screen. He was right. Its shape was far too regular to have been created by the elements.

'Come on,' insisted the Doctor, as he opened the

main door. 'That's where we're going!'

And without another word he was gone. Peri reluctantly followed, wondering why they were walking when they had the TARDIS. But if she were to play his foil, his Watson, then she would have to learn to repress her own doubts and forebodings.

She only hoped she wouldn't live, or worse still, die regretting it.

Their test completed, Romulus and Remus had been taken to an area in the safe house where they could rest.

Lounging on comfortable couches, they examined the small, black spots created when Azmael had taken possession of their memories.

Although the drug had loosened its grip even further, there were still enormous gaps in their ability to remember, and it frightened the twins.

But what had frightened them even more was the appearance of Mestor. Never in the whole of their short lives had they seen anything quite so grotesque.

Mestor the Magnificent was nearly two metres tall. Everything about him was ugly – even to other gastropods. Unlike the slugs found on Earth, Mestor stood upright, using his tail as a large foot. To aid his balance, he had grown two small, spindly legs, so that when he walked it was necessary for him to gyrate his body from side to side.

The sight wasn't a beautiful one.

Such were the large rolls of fat that covered his body that everything wobbled as he moved. So instead of a neat, mincing gait, he appeared to undulate, like a large beached walrus, desperately struggling to regain the sea.

Apart from his legs, he had also grown two tiny arms and hands which resembled the forequarters of a Tyrannosaurus Rex. And as with that particular dinosaur, they served no useful function, except when he spoke. Then he would gesticulate with them, prodding the air to emphasis a special point.

His face, what there was of it, was humanoid in form. As he did not have a neck, head or shoulders, the features had grown where what would have been the underside of a normal slug's jaw. As though to add to the peculiarity of a gastropod with a human face, the features were covered in a thin membrane.

When Romulus and Remus had first caught sight of him, they thought he had swallowed someone and that the face of the victim was protruding through the skin covering his gullet.

For all we know, they could have been right.

If Mestor had simply been an enormous slug, content to nibble at the vegetation around him, then he would have proved to be nothing more than a curiosity capable of devouring forests.

But there was a little more to him than that.

Not only did he possess an intelligence that would have put to shame the finest brains on Earth, but also a desire to dominate those around him. And like all dictators, he was none too concerned how he achieved it.

Therefore he had kidnapped the twins.

Romulus and Remus Sylvest sat on their couches and contemplated on whether they had a future. If they were to stay alive, they reasoned, they would have to continue to co-operate, as it was only a matter of time before they were rescued.

At least, that's what they hoped.

The boys fell into silence as Drak entered the room carrying a tray of food. Gratefully they accepted the simple meal, devouring it greedily. They had forgotten how hungry they were.

If Archie and Nimo Sylvest had been present, they would not have believed the twins were their children. Gone were the arrogance and the overbearing desire to be the constant centre of attention. They had even eaten their food without comment, unlike at home, when mealtimes became grotesque competitions about who could be the fastest or messiest eater.

Fear may not be the best regime to form and mould children's characters, but in the short time they had been Azmael's prisoners, Romulus and Remus Sylvest had grown up a great deal.

The only question was, would they remain alive to enjoy the benefit of that development?

Azmael yawned and stretched. For him, it too had been a hard day, but unlike the twins, he could not afford the luxury of sleep. Instead he would have to be content with a brief sojourn in the revitalising modulator.

This is a machine not unlike a matter transporter, in as much as it breaks down the molecular structure of the body. Instead of then transporting it to a pre-set destination, the modulator bombards the atoms of the body with Ferrail rays. This induces a feeling of well being and contentment. Although no substitute for natural sleep, it does allow a person without time for sleep to continue working at maximum efficiency for a short period of time. Abuse of the machine can, of course, also induce death, as Professor Zarn, its inventor, found out.

Professor James Zarn enjoyed life very much. Although he was a gifted molecular engineer, his main interest was going to parties. Inevitably on such occasions, he drank too much Voxnic, and as he went to parties seven nights a week, he lived with a permanent, mind-splitting hangover.

Awakening one morning and feeling particularly wretched, he decided it was time to do something about it. A man of his ability, he concluded, should be able to find a cure for the common hangover. Several weeks later he had built the first working revitalising modulator.

Much to his delight the machine not only massaged away his hangovers, but also revitalised him, allowing him to increase his party going. As he no longer lived by day with the permanent side-effects of Voxnic poisoning, his performance at work had also risen to new heights.

In the year 2310 AD he won the coveted Astral-Freed award for his contribution towards the eradication of space plague. Space plague was a particularly nasty disease carried by a tiny flea which lived exclusively in the hold of intergalactic balk freighters. It could leap, vertically, exactly one metre ninety, which by that year was the eye level of the average humanoid male.

No-one knew why it had evolved to leap that precise height, as no-one knew why it would then spit a fine, sticky substance into the eye of the chosen host.

But it did. And the effect was devastating.

As the flea's spittle entered the blood-stream, the victim would become relaxed, friendly and agreeable. He would stop arguing with his fellow crew members, preferring to co-exist affably. Worse still, he would become indifferent to his bonus – the only reason anyone undertook the mind-numbing work in the first place – preferring to coast along at his own relaxed pace.

Even worse than that, an infected person was unable to lie. Therefore when his ship docked, he would willingly declare any illegal cargo being carried. Point out the deliberate errors in the manifest. Report the captain for any illegal moves or shortcuts he had taken that might have endangered life or his ship. In fact, tell the precise, literal truth.

As every established and developing planet depended upon intergalactic trade to survive, the 'truth tellers', or space plague victims, became more and more embarrassing to the authorities. No-one wanted the enquiries the space plague victims provoked. On the other hand, the authorities, if they were to maintain their own credibility, couldn't ignore reported illegal activity, and were forced to investigate every allegation. This often necessitated impounding the ship until the enquiry had finished.

It was not long before a sizeable portion of the balk freighter fleet was out of action.

Even those who had managed to keep flying found it difficult to crew their ships. No-one wanted the work unless they could engage in a little smuggling. Their desire wasn't to make a vast fortune, but simply to add a little excitement to the voyage. It was also a game every crew member and custom officer enjoyed.

Then along came Professor Zarn and his team. By developing a flea that could jump three metres, then releasing it aboard the infested freighters, he immediately solved the problem. As the super fleas bred with the ordinary ones, they produced offspring that naturally jumped higher. Those that didn't brain themselves on the ceiling were able to spit to their hearts' content at nothing in particular, being a good half metre above the head of the average humanoid. The plague was soon over and everything could return to how it was before.

As stated, Professor Zarn won the Atral-Freed award for his efforts. Not only did he gain a great deal of prestige, but also a lot of money, which the foolish man insisted on spending on even bigger, longer and more outrageous parties.

One night, while more than usually under the influence of Voxnic, Zarn decided to freshen himself up a little with a session in his revitalising modulator.

Unfortunately, he took into the machine a bottle of Voxnic.

Nowadays the principles governing the modulator are fully understood, but at that time it wasn't known that two things act rather strangely under the influence of Ferrail rays.

The first is Voxnic; the second is glass.

When Zarn had finished his session in the machine, the door opened automatically. But instead of the revitalised Professor, there was nothing to be seen but an enormous bottle of Voxnic.

What had happened was this. When the Professor and Voxnic had been atomised, the Ferrail rays had caused the molecules of the alcoholic beverage to become hostile. Each Voxnic molecule had lined up with one of the Professor's, absorbed it and then used the sudden intake of energy to reproduce an exact copy of itself. Therefore, when the process was completed, there was a great deal of cloned Voxnic and no Zarn.

The bottle had enlarged itself in a similar way.

The saddest thing of all was that the bottle was discovered by a particularly drunken group of the Professor's guests, who drank it dry without a second thought.

This, of course, wouldn't happen to Azmael, partly because he knew about Zarn's unfortunate accident, but mainly because there wasn't any Voxnic in the safe house.

Cautiously, the elderly Time Lord entered the revitalising modulator, sealed the door behind him and set the control for sterilisation. It was vital that the atmosphere in the modulator was free of all foreign bodies, as the presence of an insect, for instance, could prove more devastating than Professor Zarn's liquid experience. To be drunk by your friends is bad enough, but to be ostracised by your social peers because you had suddenly the head and habits of a veedle fly (see Masters and Johnson's *Social and Sexual Life of the Veedle Fly* for the disgusting details of its behaviour pattern) would be too much.

With the cleansing process complete, Azmael set the timer to four minutes, switched on the master control and listened as the machine purred into life. Then slowly, very slowly, his body began to dissolve into a billion spheres of dancing red and white lights which glittered and sparkled as they swirled around the modulator.

The master control clicked automatically and the bombardment of Ferrail rays began. The relief of Azmael's tired molecules was instant. Although reduced to his component parts, Azmael's conscious mind remained active, allowing him to enjoy the refreshing experience as it occurred.

As the Ferrail rays continued their relaxing work,

the elderly Time Lord considered staying in the modulator forever. There were worse ways, he reckoned, of spending life than being gently pummelled and massaged into an oblivion of ecstasy. Outside the machine was only heartache, frustration, anger and disappointment. Why not leave it there? he thought. Inside the modulator he was safe, happy secure.

But he was wrong.

At first he paid no attention to the minute deviation in the purr of the machine. He had no reason to. It had done it many times before. After all, it was quite old and in need of servicing.

Even when he became aware of a strong smell, not unlike that of rotting vegetation, he still paid little attention. It wasn't until the odour had developed into a near stench that he began to worry.

But then it was too late.

Unable to leave the modulator until the timer had run its course, Azmael concentrated with all his effort to eradicate the nauseating sensation. But the harder he tried, the more powerful the presence became.

Then as suddenly as the smell had arrived, it was gone. Slowly, Azmael allowed himself to relax. As he did, he began to feel a familiar but unpleasant sensation – the presence of another consciousness in his own mind.

It was Mestor!

Poor Azmael. The only place he ever felt safe and alone had been violated by the thing he hated most.

'I know you're here,' said the Time Lord nervously.

There was a loud harsh intake of breath and the sickly, sibilant voice of Mestor began to bombard his mind.

The gastropod was, as always, angry. He had expected an all out attack by the Earth authorities, which had not materialised. This delay had meant a waste of vital time and Mestor wanted Azmael to suffer as it was his carelessness that had first led the now destroyed starfighters to Titan Three.

Even though the gastropod now knew that the Earth authorities had been horrified by the sudden loss of six of their finest and deadliest warships, and that they had recalled all their patrols in anticipation of an attack on the planet, he still had to exercise his revenge.

The attack continued until Azmael felt he was about to die.

But Mestor was not a fool. He still needed Azmael in one piece. As he sensed the Time Lord's mind crumbling, he withdrew, leaving what felt like a screaming silence in the old man's head. This was, for a moment, almost as painful as the verbal onslaught.

As the modulator came to the end of its timed cycle, the automatic control clicked once more and the door of the machine slid silently open. Azmael, looking and feeling more wretched than when he had entered, staggered out.

As he lowered himself into an easy chair, Noma and Drak entered. 'We are to return to Jaconda,' he said, trying to hide the strain in his voice.

Noma and Drak exchanged a furtive glance.

'Orders of Mestor. We are to leave at once.'

'But there is importance maintenance to be done on the ship,' said Drak.

'It must be done in flight. Now make the ship ready!'

Drak and Noma bowed, neither of them very pleased at the sudden change of plan, whether the order had come directly from Mestor or not.

7

The Reunion

Long skeletal shadows stretched across the surface of Titan Three, as the blue star, known as Singos Forty-Two, seemed to perch on its horizon, like an oval Humpty Dumpty on a wall. Soon it would be gone, its duty to spread light and warmth on the far side of the barren planet.

Peri had never seen a blue sun before and wished that the circumstances under which she was watching it were more agreeable.

The hump the Doctor had spotted on the scanner-screen in the TARDIS had proved elusive, and with the light rapidly failing, would probably remain so.

The wind had also grown colder and stronger and had started to whip the grey surface dust into mini dunes.

The thought of spending the night in the open did not appeal to Peri, for she knew that once the sun had set, they would not be able to find their way back to the TARDIS. She crouched down, embraced herself and gave a little shiver. Already the bottom edge of the sun had slipped below the horizon, giving the appearance of having been subjected to the efforts of a massive eraser.

Peri shivered again as a tiny avalanche of grit and pebbles cascaded down a nearby rock face. Cautiously she looked up and saw the Doctor, perched on top of a hillock, scanning the horizon like an Apache warrior.

Since leaving the TARDIS, the Doctor had abandoned his Sherlock Holmes persona, been Hern the Hunter for five minutes, someone called Musk, who Peri gathered was considered to be the greatest explorer in the known universe, and something resembling a country squire on a brisk walk around his estate.

The light continued to fade.

Suddenly there was a loud shout and Peri thought the Doctor had fallen. Frantically her eyes searched the rock face for his broken body, but saw that he was still on his rocky summit, this time statue-like, pointing westward into the fast disappearing sun.

Peri followed the direction in which the finger was pointing, but could see nothing but more rocky outcrops.

With the speed and agility of a practised mountain goat, the Time Lord bounded down from his observation point and set off across the bleak landscape, intent on stalking whatever he had seen. Brushing the grey surface dust from her clothes, Peri followed.

Although only walking, the Doctor seemed to be covering the ground at an enormous speed. Peri's efforts to catch him up were not helped by the impractical high-heeled boots she was wearing, which were constantly snagged by the uneven terrain.

As the Doctor disappeared around the edge of an outcrop of rock, Peri became a little panicky. She knew that to lose him now could cost her life. Desperately she broke into a run, thoughts of sprained or broken ankles vanished from her mind.

As she rounded the outcrop herself, Peri saw the now stationary Time Lord silhouetted against the receding sun. He seemed transfixed by something ahead of him. It wasn't until Peri drew alongside the Doctor that she saw the enormous freighter half hidden in a ravine. To one side, on higher ground, was the dome they had seen from the TARDIS.

Again, without speaking, the Doctor moved off, but to his companion's surprise, neither towards the ship or dome, but to a point mid-way between.

Peri tottered after him, again cursing her foolish footwear. She wanted to cry out and ask the Doctor for help, but she doubted he would hear her as he had now started to scratch at a pile of rocks, like a dog searching for a buried bone.

Quickly, he demolished the pile and Peri could see there was a metal trap door set into the ground. How the Doctor knew it was there Peri would never know, but what was beneath it she was about to find out.

Brushing the last of the grey dust from a small panel set into the trap door, the Doctor felt round its edge and seemed to flick something. Instantly the tiny panel popped open and the Time Lord pressed a sequence of buttons housed in the cavity beneath it.

Slowly, stiffly, painfully, the heavy metal sheet slid back on rusty runners to reveal a dimly lit passage below.

This time the Doctor waited for his companion, helping her descend the steps into what she could now see was some sort of service duct.

Cautiously, she looked around at the heavy pipes

and cables mounted on the walls. If the Doctor had bothered to tell her, she would have learnt that it was a supply tunnel between the dome and the landing pad.

Instead, the Doctor ran off towards the dome, Peri following, her high heeled boots echoing on the concrete floor.

If the Doctor had also bothered to mention the ducting was also a walkway, Peri might have advised caution. Instead, all she could do was scream as Noma and Drak stepped from an alcove, handguns levelled ready to fire.

Surprised, Azmael looked up as the heavy, reinforced door that separated the ducting from the main area of the dome slid open, and the Doctor and Peri were bundled in.

'Hi,' said Peri with a large grin, trying to appear like a lost tourist who had inadvertently wandered onto private property. But inside her head, she was terrified.

On the other hand, the Doctor seemed totally indifferent to his situation. Casually, he gazed around the room until his eye settled on the revitalising modulator. It had been years since he had seen such a machine, and he suddenly had the overwhelming urge to use it.

'Where have you come from?' said Azmael, crossing to the Doctor.

'I've no idea,' he said, distractedly, his eye fixed firmly on the modulator. 'But I'd love a go in your machine.'

A hard blow from Noma's gun diverted the Doctor's attention.

'Where have you come from?' Azmael repeated.

For the first time, since entering the room, the Doctor brought his full attention to bear on his interrogator. Although a thick, swirling bank of fog separated his conscious mind from his memory, a tiny, distant, flashing beacon seemed to penetrate the dense void, telling him there was something rather familiar about the face before him.

'What are you doing here?' said the mouth belonging to the face.

Peri looked at the Doctor, hoping he had an acceptable answer.

'I won't ask you again.'

Noma pressed his gun against the Doctor's head. Even this didn't prompt a reply as he was still trying to decipher what the beacon was trying to tell him.

'The Doctor's unwell,' said Peri desperately.

'Then you tell me why you're here.' Azmael now sounded tired rather than stern.

'We're pilgrims . . .' she said.

Noma sniggered.

'It's true. We're here in search of peace –'

Interrupting, Noma snapped. 'They're spies. Kill them!'

'What I'm telling you is the truth.' Again Peri looked at the Doctor, praying he would support what she was saying, but he didn't seem interested.

'As I've said, the Doctor isn't a well man. He needs a place to meditate . . .' Peri cursed herself for sounding so unconvincing. 'We were looking for a suitable cave when we stumbled into your service duct.'

Azmael eyed the Doctor's gawdy jacket, then the blouse and skirt Peri was wearing. He had met many pilgrims in his time. All of them had appeared a little mad, but none had allowed their spiritual exuberance to spill into their sartorial trappings in quite the way these two had.

Perhaps Noma was right, Azmael considered. Perhaps they should die. There was too much at stake to risk keeping them alive.

'I know you!' the Doctor suddenly blurted. The beacon he had spent so much effort and time deciphering now made sense. 'As I live and breathe – Azmael!' The words trumpeted around the room like a fanfare.

The elderly Time Lord looked both confused and embarrassed as the Doctor bounded forward and grasped his hand.

'You old dog,' he said, shaking Azmael's hand with the same enthusiasm a canine wags it tail. 'What in the name of wonder are you doing here?'

Turning to Peri, he continued. 'This is my old friend and mentor, the Master of Jaconda!'

Azmael snatched his hand back. 'I am nothing of the kind! I never saw you in my life!'

The Doctor laughed. 'Forgive me, my dear friend. Of course you don't recognise me. I've regenerated twice since our last meeting.'

He grabbed Azmael's hands and pressed them to his chest.

'There you are. Two hearts that beat as one! I am a Time Lord – just as you are.'

That, Azmael couldn't deny, as the rhythmic pulsing of the twin hearts confirmed.

'And if you still pretend not to know me, let me remind you of our last meeting. That last night. You drank like twenty giants, and I pushed you in the fountain to sober you up.'

Azmael allowed a tiny smile to flicker across his lips.

He recalled the night only too well. They had laughed, drank and loved as though it had been their last day alive. He also recalled that the Doctor, as always, was without money, and he had had to pay for their joint self-indulgence.

Nodding, Azmael said, 'I must concede, you are who you say.'

The Doctor let out a loud cheer and fondly embraced his friend.

'But . . .' he added sternly, breaking away from the Doctor's grasp, 'this is not a good time to have met.'

'Whyever not?'

Azmael related the grim details concerning Mestor, the occupation of his planet and how he had kidnapped the twins.

When the story was finished, the Doctor shook his head sadly. 'Let me help you.'

'You can't.'

'Don't be absurd. Think of it – the two of us together. What an infallible combination!'

Azmael didn't agree. 'You were always full of good intentions. But I cannot risk your interference now. The destruction of Mestor is something I must do alone.'

The Doctor looked confused. 'What does that mean?'

'You will remain here . . . You will have warmth, light, considerable comfort . . . And something to keep you busy,' he added, indicating the main door.

The Doctor glanced at the portal, uncertain what he meant.

'As we leave, I shall scramble the locks of both the main door and the one to the ducting. Between them, they have twenty million million possible combinations. Even with your agile brain, my dear Doctor, I think it will take you more than a little time to sort either of them out.'

Without protest, the Doctor and Peri were secured in a small room while Azmael prepared to leave. As they had been led to their cell, Azmael had called out, 'If it's any comfort, Doctor, I too have fond memories of that evening by the fountain.'

The Doctor had found the statement somewhat ironic. If friendship added up to nothing more than fond memories, the universe didn't stand a chance. Friendship had to be a living, positive force if it were to have any value.

Perhaps Azmael was distressed by his revenge against Mestor. Perhaps he needed to feel he could handle it alone.

But alone the individual is nothing. It is only with loving friends that there is a positive living future.

Still prostrate on the floor of the TARDIS console room, Lieutenant Hugo Lang woke with a sudden start and looked around at the unfamiliar surroundings.

Gradually, as though not to frighten or shock, the memories of recent events slowly trickled back into his mind, and he felt wretched.

In the space of a few hours, both his squadron and his career had been shot down in flames.

Slowly, Hugo climbed to his feet and made his way to the double doors that should have led to freedom, but they were locked.

Cautiously he looked around him, wondering where the Doctor had gone, if he were a prisoner, or what would happen to him next. The care and skill that had gone into tending his wounds seemed to suggest that the owner of the TARDIS didn't want him dead.

At least not for the time being.

Hugo felt the bruising on his sore neck and suddenly felt very tired. To die, he thought, might not be a bad thing. At least he wouldn't have to face a court martial.

Slowly, he slid down the double doors until he was seated on the floor. The drowsiness that filled his mind was beginning to take the upper hand.

Bewildered and confused, he fell asleep.

Awake, but just as confused, the Doctor examined the lock sealing the main door of the dome. True to his word, Azmael had scrambled the electronic circuitry on his departure.

At first, the Doctor had been confident that he could sort out the jumble fairly quickly, but closer examination had shown otherwise. The possible combinations to operate the lock were even greater than Azmael had suggested.

Meanwhile, Peri, who had resigned herself to the fact that the dome would be her home for the rest of her natural life, had started to explore.

The first room she had discovered was the kitchen, complete with adjoining storeroom which contained enough food to keep a schoolful of hungry children sated for a millennium.

The delight of discovering that they wouldn't starve to death was somewhat dampened by the sight of the cooker. To say that an honours degree in theoretical engineering was necessary to successfully operate it, would have been an exaggeration. To observe that the controls resembled the flight deck of Concorde would not only have been clichéd, but would also have been untrue. But to Peri, who had never even grasped the fundamentals of the microwave oven, learning to fly Concorde would have proved easier than learning how to boil water on such a monster.

Deciding that the Doctor would have to do the cooking, but then remembering how badly he did it, Peri left the kitchen feeling rather depressed.

The sight of the bedrooms, laboratories and greenhouse (the purpose of which was to provide the dome with fresh vegetables) lifted her spirits slightly. The library, considered the best this side of Magna Twenty-eight, lifted her spirits even more.

To die in the dome, she thought, wouldn't be a bad thing after all. At least she wouldn't die ignorant.

And when she discovered the wine cellar, she also knew she wouldn't die sober.

Peri continued her tour of inspection, passing through the power plant, workshops and a compact cinema equipped to show film, video and many other visual mediums she had never seen before.

It wasn't until she entered the last corridor that her heart really sank. Before her was a door with a purple flashing light above it. Written on the door was the legend: SELF-DESTRUCT CHAMBER. NO UNAUTHORISED PERSONNEL ALLOWED ENTRY.

Not stopping to consider whether she was authorised or not, Peri pushed open the unlocked door. Inside the room she was greeted by a massive console, which flashed and winked reminding her whimsically of the last high school prom she had attended.

After examining the console more closely, all humour evaporated from her spirit and she felt sick. The device had been set to explode.

At first the Doctor didn't recognise the sound of Peri calling, being too intent on solving the problem of the lock. But as the calling became more insistent, he abandoned his task and shuffled off.

On arriving at the self-destruct chamber, the Doctor soon confirmed that Peri's panic was fully justified and, if the timer was accurate, it was to explode in the next few minutes.

Quickly, the Time Lord set about trying to deactivate the device, but soon learnt why whoever had set it hadn't bothered to lock the door on leaving. The unit was sealed, safe from interfering fingers, including the Doctor's.

'What do we do now?' said Peri urgently.

'Find another way of getting out of here. And very soon!'

As they entered the main area, the Doctor crossed to the revitalising modulator and started to fiddle with its control unit.

'What are you doing?' demanded Peri.

'You must remain absolutely quiet,' snapped the Doctor. 'I need all my concentration.'

At least he sounded sane. Peri was concerned that the discovery of the self-destruct device might have proved too much and induced another change of personality. So far it hadn't. But how would fiddling with what looked like a glass box help them to escape?

The Doctor continued to work, rapdily reducing the control to a mass of wires and printed circuits. With increased speed, he set about removing several modular units from the main console.

After careful examination of the units, his face lit up. 'I can do it, Peri! I can do it!'

'Do what, though?'

'Get us out of here!'

Quickly he carried the units to the revitalisation chamber and started to connect them to the dismembered control panel, using wire Peri was ordered to steal from anywhere she could.

As he worked, the recurring question constantly came into his mind. Why had Azmael, at one time his greatest friend, set the self-destruct unit to explode?

The more he thought, the less sense it seemed to make.

Putting aside their friendship, Azmael must have known it would have taken weeks to break out of the dome. Whatever Azmael had planned, he would have had plenty of time to carry it out with little fear of the Doctor's interference.

The Time Lord worked on, his old energy and presence of mind having returned. He felt a new man. He only hoped that his fresh inner self would have time to mature and mellow. To be atomised on a barren, miserable planet, whose only claim to fame was that its atmosphere created feelings of melancholia, was not the way he intended to say farewell to the universe.

When not cannibalising machinery for its wire, Peri constantly flitted back and forwards to the self-destruct chamber to check the timer.

Four minutes, it said.

As she returned to the Doctor with this particularly depressing piece of news, he ordered her to enter the revitalising modulator.

'Why?'

'Just get in,' the Doctor insisted.

'But what will happen to me?'

The Doctor paused for thought. He was fairly certain what he had done would work, therefore wasting time explaining the principles of something Peri wouldn't understand seemed unnecessary. On the other hand, if he had been mistaken in any part of his wiring, she would be atomised the moment he pressed the master control.

The Doctor's dilemma was to tell or not to tell.

Under more normal circumstances he would have been more than happy to explain what was about to happen, but with less than four minutes before the self-destruct device exploded, there wasn't really the time.

There was also the possibility that Peri would resist entering the modulator cabinet if she knew the truth. If she stopped to argue, and they ran out of time, she would die anyway.

So what was the point of an explanation? he thought. But what confused him even more was why he was bothering to convince himself when death was almost imminent.

Quickly, the Doctor pushed the complaining Peri into the machine and slammed the door. He then made some rapid calculations, pressed the master switch and watched his panic-stricken friend dematerialise.

What the Doctor had done was really quite simple. As explained, the function of a revitalising modulator is precisely the same as a matter transporter, only it doesn't send you anywhere. To convert the machine into a transporter requires two things: a directional beam locater (i.e. a way of telling the machine where you want to go) and a transmission sequence (i.e. a way of sending – through time and space – what you've reduced to molecular globules).

By cannibalising various bits from the main console, the Doctor had managed to build or, more accurately, cobble together, the necessary components.

Whether they worked remained to be seen. Although Peri had dematerialised, she could in fact have been anywhere, in any condition, and that included being dead. But wherever she was and whatever state she was in, the Doctor would soon be joining her.

As the timer on the self-destruct device entered the last sixty seconds of its countdown, the Time Lord entered the revitalising modulator, set the controls and waited.

Nothing happened.

Frantically he checked the wiring for loose connections but found nothing. He then checked the master control – again nothing.

The countdown was now into its last thirty seconds.

As quickly as his shaking hands and panic-stricken mind would allow, the Doctor carefully rechecked his handywork, but still couldn't find the fault.

Finally, fraught with frustration and anger, he allowed his natural instinct as a trained and experienced scientist to take over. With all the energy and passion of a lecherous stallion he gave the revitalising modulator the heftiest kick the weight and strength of his leg would allow.

If that didn't work, then nothing would.

Again the Doctor clambered into the cabinet, sealed the door and threw the main switch. This time he was reduced to a sea of sparkling light, then he slowly faded.

It had worked!

No sooner had he gone than the timer on the self-destruct machanism reached zero, made an electrical connection and exploded, causing the building to vaporise.

Gone was the finest library this side of Magna

Twenty-eight. Gone was the most complicated cooker ever built in the history of the universe. Gone were the ghosts of the demented souls who had built and orginally occupied the dome. Gone was the computer containing their last, tortured literary jottings.

Gone was everything to do with the dome on Titan Three.

It its place appeared a large, deep crater which was soon filled with grey dust.

Meanwhile at the TARDIS, two areas of space were filled by the Doctor and Peri materialising in the console room.

Bemused and a little insulted, as neither of the sudden arrivals even bothered to say hello, Lieutenant Hugo Lang watched as the Time Lord and his companion scuttled about the console room, flicking switches, pressing buttons and generally getting in each other's way.

'What are you doing?' he said at last.

The Doctor glanced at the intergalactic policeman and, for a moment, wondered who he was. Seeing Hugo's confused look, Peri piped: 'Going to Jaconda.'

'Why?'

'Do you always ask so many questions?' snapped the Doctor.

'I'm a policeman. It's an occupational disease.'

'Then find a cure for it. We have work to do.'

And with that said, the Doctor pressed the dematerialisation switch and the time rotor juddered into motion.

8

Jaconda the Beautiful!

Azmael sat on the bridge of his freighter and furtively brushed a tear from his eye. Displayed on the monitor before him was a computer analysis of the explosion that had occured shortly after their departure from Titan Three.

Next to him stood the twins who were bristling with indignation. They had just witnessed a heated conversation between Azmael and Noma which had made them very angry.

Although they had not met the Doctor and Peri, the news of the way their lives had been casually wasted by Noma had hurt and outraged them. Although part of their anger was motivated by the fear that they too might be disposed of in an equally off-hand way, they had also felt a genuine compassion, fury and indignation that, until now, had been quite alien to their immature minds.

What, in reality, had happened was that Noma had secretly informed Mestor of the Doctor's arrival. Concerned by the intervention of a second Time Lord, Mestor had ordered Noma to destroy the Doctor, Peri and the safe house.

Also, Mestor was still concerned that once the Earth authorities had rediscovered their nerve, they would launch an attack. As already proven, Azmael had shown a rather casual attitude towards covering his tracks. With the safe house destroyed, the trail to Jaconda would end on Titan Three.

Although Azmael tried to explain this, the twins weren't interested and remained resolute as to who was really to blame. As leader of the group, Azmael was responsible for the activities of each member.

As Romulus and Remus continued their verbal attack, Drak came to the elderly Time Lord's rescue with an offer of more food. Reluctantly, the twins gave into their baser need and allowed themselves to be bustled away.

Once gone, Azmael could no longer hold back the tears. Not since the death of his dear wife had he felt such grief and despair. As he sobbed, he wondered how many more good people would have to die before Jaconda would be rid of Mestor.

Although his tears were mainly for the Doctor, they also contained a few of self pity. It was becoming obvious to Azmael that he was losing his grip on the situation. Up until recently he had always been confident that ultimately he could defeat Mestor. Yet lately the creature seemed to grow stronger, more confident and inventive by the day.

The cloud Mestor had sent to destroy the starfighters was proof of that. The technology and imagination necessary for such a feat was beyond Azmael's comprehension. Even Mestor's ability to thought-read had grown more effective, making it more and more difficult for Azmael to plot and plan. It had almost reached the point where the Time Lord felt nowhere was safe from the prying awareness of his arch-enemy.

Although the twins had been harsh and brutal in their attack on Azmael, they had in one respect, been absolutely right. He was the President of Jaconda and the responsibility for the safety and well-being of his people did lie with him. If he wasn't capable of fulfilling his duties, then it was right that he should resign and leave others to try and succeed in their own way.

But who would replace him? It was a thought that had constantly crossed his mind.

When Mestor and his army of gastropods had emerged from hibernation, many socially important Jacondans had rushed to join him before an angry shot had been fired. Even those who had bravely fought soon surrendered once they realised the war could drag on for years.

Civil servant, politician, merchant and financier alike had all declared their allegiance and had openly collaborated. A few had smiled to deceive their conqueror, whilst quietly working to defeat him, but they had soon been betrayed and murdered.

It is said by cynics that the shortest list of war heroes in the whole of the universe is to be found on Jaconda. Azmael learnt, to his misery, that there was more than a grain of truth in that observation.

Of course, Jacondan historians deny this, declaring that Jaconda exists to trade peacefully. It never seemed to occur to them that only *free* people can trade *peacefully*, and however much war may be despised, it is sometimes necessary, especially when invaded by a monster determined to destroy everything the planet is supposed to hold sacred.

When the Seedle warriors had come to Vitrol Minor in search of Azmael, he had been helped beyond the call of any individual's duty. While the warriors had set about murdering the populace, he had been smuggled off the planet by brave people indifferent to their own personal safety. Azmael hadn't needed to ask for such sacrifice, as each individual had offered their help willingly, only too aware that subjection to evil creates and feeds further evil.

Perhaps it was too much to expect the Jacondans to be as brave as those on Vitrol Minor, but it saddened him that the people of his adopted planet had such little self respect and awareness of their own freedom and dignity.

Carefully, Azmael dried his eyes. It was time to stop remembering. Whether the people of Jaconda wanted to fight or not, was up to them. As far as he was concerned, Mestor had to die, as he had brought nothing to the planet but famine, suffering and death.

But alone, he wondered, how effective would he be?

As the TARDIS had made its way towards Jaconda, the Doctor had waxed lyrical about the beauty of the planet, of its lush meadows, its wooded countryside, its easy-going, friendly people.

The reality proved somewhat different.

As the Doctor and his party stepped from the TARDIS, they couldn't believe the devastation before them. It was as though a nuclear explosion had taken place.

The ground was scorched and black. What was left of the trees looked like skeletons that had been gnawed and ravaged by sharp-toothed scavengers. In spite of the barrenness of the planet, a heavy obnoxious stench hung in the air, reminiscent of a particularly unpleasant compost heap.

Although the Jacondan sun shone, it seemed to offer little warmth, as though the desolation absorbed the life-giving heat, jealous that it was unable to utilise its energy, but determined no-one else should enjoy it.

Cautiously, the Doctor moved around, examining first the stripped trunks of the trees, then the heavy, impacted soil. Everything was covered in a thick, mucus which hardened into a concrete-like substance, making close examination difficult.

As the Doctor continued his exploration, he caught sight of the frightened, timid face of a child staring at him from a nearby hill. The Time Lord waved and smiled, but the boy scurried off to whatever passed for safety in such a lifeless place.

Peri and Hugo watched the painfully thin child and wondered how anyone managed to survive in such a place.

'Can't we help him?' asked Peri anxiously.

The Doctor shook his head. 'The only way we can help him is to destroy what has caused this desolation.'

'That will hardly help him survive,' snapped Peri. 'He needs food now!'

Ignoring her outburst, the Doctor continued to examine the terrain. He knew only too well that the child would probably die, but where there was one hungry boy, there would be many others in just as much need. Although there was food aboard the TARDIS, there wouldn't be enough to keep anyone alive longer than their current condition would permit. The Doctor knew this and considered their time better spent searching out Mestor.

'What caused this devastation?' asked Hugo, crumbling a dry, lifeless twig.

'Gastropods...'

Peri and Hugo looked at each other. *Slugs did this?*

'Giant gastropods...' added the Doctor, reading their thoughts. 'Look at the slime trails if you don't believe me.'

As they returned to the TARDIS, the Doctor briefly related the myths and legends surrounding the gastropods of Jaconda.

It went something like this: Hundreds of years earlier, a then queen of the planet had offended the sun god, who in his revenge had forced her to give birth to a half-human, half-slug creature. (The reasons for this rather unpleasant retribution weren't certain.) Before long the gastropod had multiplied until its offspring had become numberless, ravaging and plundering the planet until every living plant had been eaten and everyone was on the verge of starvation.

It wasn't until the planet had been devastated that the sun god relented and sent a drought to destroy the slugs.

'But that's all myth,' said Peri. 'Outside is *real* devastation!'

The Doctor started to set the navigational co-ordinates. 'As you well know,' he said, glancing over his shoulder, 'myths are often embroidered stories that contain more than a grain of truth. Forget about sun gods and offending queens. Just concentrate on the fact that somehow giant slugs found their way to Jaconda.'

'But you said they had died out.'

'My dear Peri, use a little of your not inconsiderable imagination. The beast itself may have died out but it seems fairly obvious that it left a heritage in the form of many clutches of eggs. Somehow they must have hatched.'

'Starting the whole cycle again?'

'Correct.'

'Pity there isn't a sun god to relent and send a drought nowadays,' said Hugo.

Peri glared at him. Why didn't he keep his mouth shut, she thought. With the current state of the Doctor's mind, all it required was such a silly suggestion to set him off again. Cautiously, Peri glanced at the Time Lord. If he had heard what had been said, he hadn't reacted.

At least not yet.

Peri hoped this indicated the Doctor was beginning to stabilise.

With the co-ordinates set, the Doctor operated the master control and the time rotor started to oscillate. If his calculations were correct, as they often were nowadays, they would soon arrive at Azmael's palace where they could delight in the company of Mestor and his friends.

From their rude, sarcastic remarks, the Doctor reckoned his companions could barely restrain their eager anticipation . . .

Upon arriving on Jaconda, Azmael had been summoned before Lord Mestor. Again he had been subjected to a ranting tirade.

This time, though, Azmael had felt doubly embarrassed, as Mestor had insisted on insulting him in front of his courtiers, many of whom had served the elderly Time Lord when he had been President. Although some remained silent, Azmael hoped as a mark of respect, many others had joined in the jeering and general abuse.

After being dismissed, Azmael dejectedly made his way back to his laboratory. There he found the twins staring through the glass wall that separated his work area from Mestor's hatchery.

Fascinated, the boys watched the technicians as they loaded gastropod eggs onto a conveyor belt system which then took them deep into the heart of the incubation area.

'So many eggs,' said Remus, noticing Azmael. 'Will they all hatch?'

The Time Lord nodded. 'And now you're going to ask me why we're breeding so many gastropod eggs when I have already said that Jocanda is on the verge of starvation?'

'Not at all,' said Romulus. 'My brother and I were wondering how our mathematical skill could possibly aid you in slug husbandry.'

'Come with me.'

Azmael led the twins to a corner of the laboratory where there was a beautifully made astronomical model of the Jacondan solar system. Pressing a button built into the base the model jerked into life.

'As you can see, there are only three planets in our solar system. The largest and nearest to our sun in Jaconda. The two other planets, Muston and Senial, are not only much smaller but are also uninhabited.'

Fascinating, thought the twins. But it was hardly an answer to their question.

'It is the intention of Mestor,' continued the Time Lord, 'to bring Muston and Senial into the same orbit as Jaconda.' He tried to make the statement sound as matter of fact as he could. 'Once the planets have adjusted to their new position, I am informed by our agronomists, we shall be able to farm them.'

The twins stared at Azmael as though he were mad. 'Have you any idea what would happen if anything were to go wrong?'

'I am assured that nothing will,' said Azmael rather stiffly.

'And what is supposed to be our part in this ridiculous plan?'

'We already have the technology to move the planets. What we require from you is the mathematical delicacy that will stabilise them once they are in their new orbit.'

'And what if we refuse to help?'

'Then I shall kill you.'

The statement was casual, unforced and the twins knew he meant it. For the first time in their dual existence they had been threatened with death. Instead of feeling hurt and outraged, they understood the pain that Azmael must be suffering. Moving the outer planets into the same orbit as Jaconda's was for him one way of trying to save his people from starvation. He was desperate to succeed. And they accepted it.

They were also aware that the scheme was a lunatic one.

Carefully, they considered what they should do. Somehow they had to stop him. The thought of dying heroically, however glamorous it may appear to the onlooker, did not appeal to them. To aimlessly throw away their lives by not co-operating would be pointless. Neither would it stop Mestor or Azmael. They would simply go ahead without them. Alive, they had power to control events. But how?

It was possible that Azmael would respond to reasoned, logical argument and the reality of events. As

Mestor started to move the first planet and the impossibility of his task became obvious, Azmael would be forced to do something. After all, to die from another planet crashing into your own is as permanent as dying from starvation.

At least, that's how they reasoned.

On the other hand, Mestor was something else. The twins wondered how much he cared about anything. If things started to go wrong, he might insist that they continue irrespective of the consequence. As he had the power to back his insistence, they could all finish up dead and with the Jacondan corner of the universe in chaos.

The twins decided they would have to play the situation by ear. Trying to make too many plans was foolish. But first they would have to gain the confidence of Azmael.

'All right...' they said as one voice. 'We'll co-operate.'

Azmael smiled. 'Your decision pleases me. Thank you.'

Then in spite of their good intentions (or was it a subconscious reaction to make their sudden conversion credible?) Romulus muttered, 'We still think you're mad.'

'Quite mad...' Remus chipped in.

'Neurotic, psychotic...'

'And despotic.'

Azmael nodded. 'You could be right. We'll just have to wait and see.'

What was referred to as Azmael's palace was, in fact, a massive citadel. It was said that parts of it were over two thousand years old, but such had been its piece-meal development that any architectual or historical value it may have once had had long since been lost. Instead, its collected buildings gracelessly sprawled down from the top of the mountain on which the original structure had been built.

Peri and Hugo were not destined to see this view of the citadel, as the Doctor had decided to materialise in one of its maze of forgotten corridors.

As the trio stepped from the TARDIS into a dingy, dank corridor, Peri heard herself saying indignantly, 'This is the seediest stately home I've ever seen.'

'You didn't expect me to materialise in the throne room?' was the sharp retort.

Peri didn't answer. Nowadays she didn't know what to expect from the Doctor. Although he seemed to have stabilised since his earlier erratic outbursts, there was still something odd and remote about him.

As they moved off along the passageway, going they knew not where, it had occurred to Hugo that if the twins were on Jaconda, he could still fulfill his mission and rescue them, thereby also saving his own career.

The more he thought about it, the more the idea excited him. He had always dreamed of being declared a hero, ever since he had joined starfighter command. His natural good looks, easy charm and ability to look good in a uniform made him, so Hugo thought, a perfect choice.

As a hero he would be able to give up flying – something that still frightened him – possibly enter politics, or specialise in appearing on the numerous chat shows that dominated the public viddy channels. The money was good, the adoration overwhelming and, most of all, it was safe.

Heroes never slipped in the ratings. As they grew older, wiser and better informed, they would transfer to the debate programmes, of which there were even more than chat shows. If Hugo proved really successful, he might even be granted the ultimate accolade, that of becoming the chairman of his very own show!

Carried away on the wings of his own fantasy, Hugo had overlooked one thing: he still had to find the twins. There was also the Doctor and Peri to consider, but Hugo had decided to dump them at the first opportunity. He didn't want to risk anyone eclipsing his success. Neither did he need the Doctor to pilot the TARDIS. Careful study of it in flight had convinced Hugo that he was capable of handling the ship alone.

As the group continued to move cautiously along the passage, Peri whispered, 'Are you sure we're going the right way?'

The Doctor nodded. 'Azmael gave me a conducted tour the last time I was here. This passage leads to his laboratory.'

As he spoke, the group became aware of a strong, pungent smell, very similar to the one that had pervaded the wasteland they had visisted earlier.

Quickly, the Doctor pushed Hugo and Peri into a deep alcove leading off the passageway.

They were no sooner in place then through the silence they heard the faint mooing and slithering of two gastropods.

As Hugo silently drew his gun, the Doctor gripped his arm and indicated that he should not use it. The risk was too great as there were bound to be armed guards nearby.

As they pressed deeper into the dark shadows which

shared the alcove with them, the two gastropods slithered by. The stench which emanated from them was so overpowering that Peri started to retch. Quickly, the Doctor placed his hand on his young companion's mouth to silence her.

With gastropods gone and their sickly smell beginning to clear, Hugo decided to take his chance. Unnoticed by the Doctor and Peri, he slipped into the main passageway, his intention to find the twins and get back to the TARDIS while the Doctor was dealing with Mestor.

Cautiously, he started to make his way along the passage, but suddenly became aware that something was dragging at his feet. Looking down, he saw that his boots were covered by a dense, sticky mucus.

As he tried to move on, Hugo realised that the mucus was beginning to set hard. Seconds later, he was stuck fast, as though someone had glued him to the floor.

'Doctor!' he called in a loud, hoarse whisper. 'I'm stuck!'

The Doctor and Peri peered into the passage and immediately saw the literal mess the pilot had got himself into.

'That's what you get for wandering off!'

'Spare me the lecture, Doctor!' Then softening his tone, he added, 'Please get me out of here!'

'Can't.'

'Why not?'

'Gastropod slime trails set like concrete.'

'You can't abandon him!' pleaded Peri.

The Time Lord prodded the thick, hard slime with the toe of his shoe. 'There's nothing I can do.'

A look of horror spread across Hugo's face. 'You

can't leave me here!'

'I can and I must. I have more important matters to attend to.'

'If those gastropods come back, they'll kill me!'

'You should have thought about that when you tried to sneak away.'

Hugo levelled his gun and took careful aim at the Doctor. 'Leave me here and I'll kill you.'

The Doctor smiled. 'Then how would you get home?'

Hugo didn't reply.

'I saw the way you were watching me when I was operating the TARDIS's controls. Looked simple, didn't it? But you'll find there is more to flying the TARDIS than pressing a few switches.'

'I'll take my chance,' growled Hugo.

'Then you'll take it alone,' interrupted Peri. 'If you kill the Doctor, I won't help you.'

Hugo considered the situation for a moment, then lowered his gun. 'I'm sorry,' he said, trying to sound like a little boy caught doing something naughty. 'I panicked. I wasn't thinking.'

'You should try it sometime,' snapped the Doctor. 'You'll find it useful. Now try pointing that gun at your feet.'

Uncertain whether the Doctor was cracking some sort of Gallifreyan joke, the young pilot looked down at his trapped boots.

'If you set your laser gun to its lowest setting you might be able to cut yourself free.'

Hugo instantly obeyed, cursing for not having thought of the idea himself. Carefully he lined the gun up with the edge of his boot and squeezed the trigger. A thin, red, perfect beam of light shot from the weapon, and slowly the hardened mucus began to buckle under the high temperature of the ray.

As Hugo worked, the Doctor whispered to Peri, 'I'm wasting valuable time.' His voice was now tense and irritable. 'I sense that something terrible is about to happen.'

Peri gazed at the strained features of the Time Lord, concerned by his sudden change of mood. 'I'm sure he won't be long.'

'But will he be quick enough?'

Peri didn't understand. Neither was she given the chance to.

'I'm off,' snapped the Doctor, and he started off along the passage, Peri following.

'Do you think it wise to go off alone when you're so agitated!' she asked.

'I am not agitated!'

Suddenly the Doctor stopped dead and Peri almost bumped into him. 'Unless you're implying I'm about to have one of my fits!'

That was precisely what Peri was implying, but thought it unwise to pursue the point. Instead she said, 'I'm concerned you may meet more gastropods. Together we might be able to defeat them. But alone you wouldn't stand a chance.'

'I have always managed alone. I was born alone. I shall die alone. I've also come to the conclusion that it is best to spend the time between those two unfortunate events alone. Do you understand?'

Peri nodded.

'Now go back to Hugo,' snapped the Doctor. 'And when he's freed himself from the mucus, take him back to the TARDIS. I don't want either of you getting in my way.'

A moment later he had mounted a much worn flight

of stone steps and, taking them two at a time, disappeared into the gloom above, watched by a confused and very worried Peri.

On reaching the top of the steps the Doctor turned into an even more miserable passage than the one he had just left. Here the hardened trails of mucus were more numerous and the Doctor increased his pace. More trails meant more gastropods and he had to find Azmael before he was discovered himself.

Up another flight of stairs, the Time Lord jogged. Along yet another bleak, dank corridor. Then quickly into an alcove and the safety of its dark shadows, as the Doctor caught sight of another gastropod. With the danger passed, he continued his quest desperately trying to remember where Azmael's laboratory was.

As the Doctor entered a large quadrangle with a corridor leading off from every corner, he was finally forced to face the fact that he was lost. To take a wrong turning now would not only lead him further away from Azmael, but deeper into the citadel and closer to being caught by Mestor's guards.

The Doctor scratched his head. What to do next? As he pondered, he heard a familiar, schoolmasterly voice echoing along the corridor nearest to him.

It was Azmael!

The Doctor broke into a run as he headed towards the pedagogic chant, delighted that his old friend was able to project his voice so well. How many times had the Doctor sat in Azmael's classroom, trying not to listen to one of his complicated lectures, only to find his deep, rolling vowel sounds breaking through the protective wall of his distracted thoughts.

This time, though, the Doctor was all ears.

As he approached the heavy wooden door, through

which the dulcet tones of his old teacher boomed, the Doctor could also hear the more squeaky, less controlled voices of the twins. Delightedly the Doctor smiled, then braced himself to enter the room.

With all the swash and buckle of a Sabatini hero, the Time Lord threw open the door and bounded in. 'Still bullying children, eh, Azmael?'

Rapidly the bemused quartet in the room turned to see who was making so much fuss and noise. *Who in the world is this fool?* their expression said.

The Doctor glanced over his shoulder to see who they were really looking at.

Then slowly, painfully, he realised they were looking at him.

Meanwhile, Hugo had managed to free himself from the hardened slime. Although Peri had protested long and forcefully, the young pilot had refused to return to the TARDIS. His mission, he had declared rather pompously, was to save the twins.

Unfortunately, Hugo had proclaimed his quest too loudly, and, as he moved off in the same direction the Doctor had taken, two Jacondan guards stepped from the shadows rendering him unconscious neatly and efficiently with the butt of their guns.

As Peri turned to run, she had come face to face with a third guard who smiled politely then twisted her arm painfully behind her back.

Once more she was a prisoner, and like the times before, she hated it!

9

End Game, Part One

Drak, who had been slouched in a corner reading a comic, was the first to move. As he got to his feet he tugged his laser pistol from its holster.

Romulus and Remus watched the Jacondan in eager anticipation of violence. But they were unlucky.

Azmael, momentarily struck dumb by the unnecessary aggression of the Doctor's arrival, located his voice, then stepped forward to greet him.

'My dear friend,' he said extending his hand. 'I'm delighted to see that you're safe.'

The Doctor, feeling less affable, responded with a mouthful of abuse. He demanded to know why Azmael had found it necessary to try and kill him.

Deciding it was time to play the diplomat, Drak stepped between the two arguing men. 'Azmael didn't know the self-destruct mechanism had been set.'

The Doctor didn't believe the Jacondan.

'He's telling the truth,' said Remus.

'It was the other man,' added Romulus. 'His name's Noma.'

The Doctor looked around the room. 'Where is he?'

'With Lord Mestor,' said Drax. 'And I wouldn't be

too quick to blame him. He was only obeying Mestor's orders.'

Azmael extended his hand again. 'I am truly delighted you survived, my dear Doctor.'

This time the hand was accepted.

'Now we must find somewhere for you to hide.'

The Doctor shook his head. 'First tell me what's going on here.'

Quickly Azmael told of Mestor's plan to move the two outer planets of the Jacondan solar system and turn them into agricultural paradises.

Silently the Doctor listened, both amazed and impressed at the boldness of the plan, until his eye fell on the astronomical model.

Followed by Azmael, the Doctor crossed to examine it more carefully. There was no need for him to ask whether the model was of the Jacondan solar system, as a small, neatly engraved plaque announced the fact.

'Is this model to scale?' enquired the Doctor.

'Of course.'

'Very interesting,' muttered the Doctor.

'Is there something wrong?'

But before the Doctor could answer, the door of the laboratory was thrown open and two guards entered, supporting a stunned Hugo.

Gently they lowered him into a chair. As they did, Noma appeared at the door. 'The Lord Mestor wishes you to exmaine the humanoid for internal damage.'

'Of course,' said Azmael crossing to Hugo.

At the same moment Noma noticed the Doctor. 'You certainly get around,' he smirked. 'I think you'd better come with me. The Lord Mestor would like a few words with you.'

'Where's Peri?' demanded the Doctor.

'Quite safe,' echoed a sickly, sibilant voice which definitely wasn't Noma's.

As the Doctor glanced around, wondering where the sound had come from, a hologram image started to form in the middle of the room.

It was Mestor, showing off again.

'Welcome to Jaconda, Doctor,' the voice hissed. 'Although I would have thought it more polite if you had announced your presence without me having to seek you out.'

'Actually I didn't come to see you. Although I'm sure you won't be disappointed in having me around,' the Doctor said casually. 'Especially as I think I can help you.'

Azmael stiffened, expecting Mestor to violently lose his temper.

'*You* help *me*?'

'That's right,' chirped the Doctor. 'Azmael has been telling me of your plan to shift the orbit of two of your planets. Very impressive.'

As he spoke, the Doctor strolled through the hologram image of Mestor, something, instinct told him, the gastropod wouldn't like.

He was right.

A sudden roar filled the laboratory, but before Mestor could follow it up, the Doctor continued. 'Mind you, moving planets isn't for amateurs, you know. The twins may possess the mathematical knowledge, but I have the empirical skill, the practical experience that will guarantee success. I mean, one false move and the planet you're trying to shift could fly off in any direction.'

He paused. If Mestor was interested in what the Doctor was saying, he would be eager to hear more. If he continued to shout and bluster, then the Doctor knew he was in trouble.

There was silence.

Although Mestor considered himself clever, the psychological strategy of bullying a victim into submission was an uninspired one. Fear, induced by bullying, can only be a useful weapon when its user can deliver the coup de grâce knowing he has nothing to lose.

Silence from a bully tells his opponent far too much.

If Mestor had been as clever as he thought he was, he would have learnt that a quieter way to domination leaves the opponent far more shattered than the loudest shout.

Not only did the Doctor know he had Mestor's interest, his silence also told him he was less certain of his skill in successfully manoeuvring the planets than he was letting on.

'Well?' the Doctor said at last. 'Are you interested in my help?'

'Why should I want you to help me?'

'I would rather you were successful in your aims, than you destroy this part of the universe.'

'You are telling the truth, Time Lord?'

The Doctor let out a high-pitched, nervous laugh he had intended to sound ironic. In spite of his confidence, the pressure was beginning to tell on him as well.

In an attempt to correct his error, the Doctor pulled his voice down a full half octave and said with as much assurance as he could muster, 'You should know. I can sense your presence in my mind.'

'Then why do you resist me?'

'I'm secretive by nature. Anyway, if you were to learn everything too soon, you would have little reason to keep me alive.'

'True, Doctor.' Mestor's voice was now hard and cold, aware that the Time Lord was playing with him. 'You may serve me, but should I sense any deception on your part, than I shall have you put to death immediately.'

'Oh, absolutely,' said the Doctor dismissively. 'But before I start work, I have one request to make.'

The Doctor mentally crossed his fingers. 'I believe you have a friend of mine prisoner.'

'The woman from Earth. She is here.'

'I shall need her to assist me.'

The hologram flickered and the Doctor feared that its disappearance would be Mestor's dismissive answer.

'I have scanned her mind. It contains little but a scant knowledge of botany and certainly nothing that would assist you in your task.'

The Doctor cleared his throat. 'When I say I require her assistance, I mean that in a metaphorical way. Her presence inspires within me a certain tranquility that is most useful if I am to do my best work.'

Again, the hologram flickered. 'Oh, very well,' said Mestor. 'You may have your intellectual prop.'

Inside his head, the Doctor gave a small cheer. If anyone was numbering the rounds, he had definitely won the first. 'I am indeed grateful, Lord Mestor.'

As he spoke, the Doctor glanced at the grey, drawn face of Azmael. The poor man looked as though he was about to collapse. 'Perhaps you could do me one last favour,' he said cheekily. 'Azmael is in need of a mild stimulant. Perhaps Peri could bring a bottle of Voxnic with her.'

There was a loud roar and the hologram disappeared.

'Incredible,' muttered Azmael. 'I've never heard anyone talk to Mestor in such a manner and live.'

'This is just the beginning,' the Doctor teased.

'The next time you do something as foolish, I would be grateful for prior warning. I'm too old to cope with this sort of strain.'

A groan from a slumped figure, perched precariously on a hard, wooden chair, served to announce that Lieutenant Hugo Lang was regaining consciousness. Drak, for ever caring and vigilant, crossed to attend to him.

In spite of his initial victory, the Doctor still felt uneasy. Something wasn't quite right. The astronomical model still worried him and, in spite of everything, Mestor had given in just a little too easily.

But before the air of triumph was allowed to fade, the Doctor ordered the guards with the exception of Drak from the laboratory. It would be difficult enough to operate knowing that Mestor could tune in whenever he wanted without having guards looking over his shoulder.

Much to everyone's amazement they left without argument. But then seconds before the Doctor had uttered his command, Mestor had ordered them to leave and find his TARDIS.

If the Doctor was planning to escape, Mestor had reasoned, he certainly wasn't going to make it easy for him.

As the Doctor, deep in thought, paced up and down the laboratory, the door opened and, clutching a large bottle of Voxnic, Peri sheepishly entered.

'Thanks for getting me out of trouble,' she mewed.

The Doctor dismissed her thanks with a wave of the hand and continued his pacing.

As he did so, Azmael, Hugo and Drak fell on the bottle of Voxnic and quickly poured and drank a large beakerful each. As they refilled their cups with more of the golden liquid, Azmael enquired if anyone else wanted a drink. The Doctor didn't answer and Peri shook her head politely.

Although the twins showed great interest, Azmael, somewhat paternally, decided they were too young, but in reality, felt his need was greater than theirs.

As Azmael downed his second beaker, the familiar glow the twins knew only too well from their father spread slowly across his face. Even Peri noticed the change and thought she might try a little herself. As she picked up the bottle, the Doctor let out a sudden shout.

'That's it! I knew there was something wrong.'

His voice sounded a little manic and it worried Peri. 'Are you all right?'

'Of course I'm all right,' he shouted, snatching up the Voxnic and taking a large mouthful. 'I'm certainly all right. It's the situation that's wrong!'

He slammed the bottle down on the table as though to enforce his statement. 'Look at this,' he said crossing to the astronomical model. 'Correct me if I'm wrong, Azmael, but you said this model was to scale.'

The elderly Time Lord nodded.

'Then look at the planets to be moved,' he said prodding each of them in turn. 'Both of them are smaller than Jaconda.'

That was obvious.

The Doctor turned to Azmael who was about to slurp his way through a third beakerful of Voxnic. 'Think of the consequences, old friend, if those planets should be brought into the same orbit as Jaconda.'

Azmael did, but nothing startling occurred to him.

'Think again,' the Doctor insisted. 'It's a matter of simple physics.'

Simple or not, Azmael still couldn't see what he was supposed to.

'Can't you give us a clue?' prompted Peri.

The Doctor thought for a moment. 'The gravitational pull of the sun on Jaconda is more or less constant. Yes?'

Peri shrugged. 'I'll take your word for it.'

'Place the two smaller planets in the same orbit as Jaconda and how long do you think they'd remain there?'

Slowly Azmael placed his beaker on the table. 'Why didn't I realise?' he stammered. 'They wouldn't last any time at all.'

'Why not?' enquired Peri.

'Because their orbit would rapidly decay and they would crash into the sun.' Azmael buried his head in his hands. 'Why, oh why didn't I think of that myself?'

The Doctor placed a reassuring arm around his old friend's shoulder. 'Your mind has been on other things.'

'But I should have known at once,' wailed Azmael. 'You're absolutely right. It's basic physics.'

'And when the planet hits the sun,' muttered Hugo, 'it'll be like the birth of a super nova.'

The Doctor glanced at Hugo as though he had forgotten he was in the room. 'That's right.'

Hugo emptied his beaker. 'Do you think Mestor knows what will happen?'

The Doctor nodded.

'Then why does he allow it?' said Peri. 'He'll be killed

too.'

The Doctor smiled at her naivety. 'I have the feeling he'll be long gone by then.'

Watched by Drak, the group settled into an atmosphere of silent depression. Yet the same question pounded through each and every brain in the room: *what did Mestor hope to achieve by deliberately destroying his own sun?*

Soon they would find out.

10

End Game, Part Two

The Doctor stared at the glass partition which separated Mestor's hatchery from the laboratory area, and allowed his mind to flick through the many pages of his long memory, hoping some half-forgotten incident might jog his inspiration into solving the current problem.

But it didn't.

All he seemed able to recall were faces and fragments of incidents, some of which he would rather have forgotten.

He recalled Jo Grant, with her soft, pretty face, framed by her always perfectly groomed, blond hair. He remembered Tegan, Leela, Zoe and Jamie. Even Turlough, the only companion who had seriously tried to kill him, flittered in and out of images of Nyssa, Romana and Liz Shaw.

But the image that danced most frequently across the history of time was that of Adric, for he performed the most grotesque caper of all, that of the Dance of Death.

Adric who, despite possessing a mathematical skill equal to the twins, had always managed to aggravate everyone aboard the TARDIS with his childish antics denying him the thing he desired most: to be loved and accepted for what he was.

It was Adric who had been killed whilst trying to divert a freighter, controlled by the Cybermen, from crashing into prehistoric Earth.

Stubborn Adric, who had refused to leave the ship and had given his life to help others.

It was this memory that the Doctor feared most. Not only had he been forced to stand helplessly by, but the boy had died without the Doctor ever being able to fully praise, help or ultimately like. It was these feelings that made Adric the saddest and most painful memory of all.

The Doctor shook his head as though trying to shake himself free of the unpleasant image. It wasn't the time to remember such things. He had more urgent problems to occupy his mind.

Slowly he refocussed his eyes so that his gaze passed through the glass partition and into the hatchery beyond.

The technicians had gone and the conveyor belt was stationary. The level of lighting had also been reduced, creating dense, eerie shadows.

The sight made the Doctor feel uneasy and he climbed to his feet, crossed to the control box situated at the side of the partition and fiddled with one of the switches.

Slowly the lights came up inside the hatchery, forcing the shadows to hide. 'What's this?'

Azmael ambled over to join the Doctor. 'Mestor's hatchery.'

'Can we get into it?'

The elderly Time Lord operated another lever on the control panel and, as the heavy partition started to rise,

Peri crossed the room and joined them.

'Why do you want to go in there?' she enquired.

'I'm curious.'

Peri glanced at Azmael and hoping for his support said: 'But do we have the time?'

If Azmael agreed with the question, he didn't care to pursue it, as he remained silent.

Neither did the Doctor answer. Something was aggravating him, gnawing at the back of his mind.

With the partition fully open, the trio entered the hatchery. As they scrambled past the conveyor belt, they entered the dark cavern which was the main incubation area. It was hot and sticky and gave off a pungent, fruity smell.

As their eyes became accustomed to the gloom, it became apparent that the cavern went on for miles. Packed around its walls were millions of eggs, each one fitting neatly and precisely into a purpose-built slot.

Cautiously, the Doctor moved to one of the racks and lifted out an egg. It was the approximate size and shape of a rugby ball and weighed about one kilo. Cupping it in his hands, the Doctor seemed to be assessing the egg, trying to work out what was wrong with it. For something was missing, something that was so natural and obvious it took the Time Lord a full minute to realise what it was.

Without comment, the Doctor handed the egg to Peri and quickly moved to another rack. Carefully he felt all the eggs housed in it, and like the first one, they were dry.

'Something wrong?' enquired Peri.

'There certainly is. If these are gastropod eggs, why are they dry? Where is the mucus, the jelly, the food which nourishes the young within?'

Peri shrugged and then looked down at the egg. It certainly was dry, but then the sort of slugs she was used to didn't come two metres high and talk!

'There's something wrong,' said the Doctor, snatching the egg from his companion. 'This may be the answer we've been looking for.'

Peri and Azmael followed as the Doctor made his way back to the laboratory area. 'I must see what's inside this egg,' he said placing it on a work bench. 'I shall need a laser cutter.'

Azmael rummaged momentarily in a cabinet and handed the Doctor what he wanted. The Doctor immediately set to work, allowing the white hot beam of light to focus on a single spot of the rubbery shell.

But nothing happened.

Strange, thought the Doctor, there must be something wrong with the cutter. But careful examination proved that it was in perfect working order. So he tried again. But still nothing happened.

'What are you trying to do?' jested Hugo. 'Hard-boil it?'

'Hardly!' The Doctor wasn't in the mood for jokes. 'The beam of the cutter is as hot as a diamond is hard. It should have at least scratched the surface.'

As the cutter continued to ineffectually blaze away at the egg, an unpleasant slurping sound was heard to come from within the shell.

The Doctor switched off the cutter as the sound grew momentarily louder and then more unpleasant.

'Is it going to hatch?' enquired Peri.

'I don't think so.'

And, as though to prove him right, the slurping sound stopped.

'The embryo only reacted to the heat,' said Azmael.

'Precisely what it's supposed to do. Only it isn't anything like hot enough yet.'

Puzzled, Hugo glanced at Peri, but she didn't understand what he was talking about either. 'You're talking in riddles, Doctor.'

'No he isn't,' said Azmael, beginning to see what the Doctor was getting at.

'Now you're *both* talking in riddles,' insisted Peri. 'What *is* going on?'

How best to explain an intuitive leap, whose inspiration stems from tiny disparate events and observations? It was possible he was wrong, but the reassurance of Azmael's concurrence made it unlikely.

The Doctor was also aware that Peri and Hugo's own scepticism wouldn't help them to believe what he was about to tell them, especially after his eccentric behaviour since his regeneration.

But did it matter? Did any of it matter? Right or wrong in his assumption, Mestor had to be stopped.

In a quiet, even voice the Doctor began to relate how and what he had concluded.

At the safe house Azmael had said that Mestor had led an original army of several hundred gastropods. Not only had they taken over Jaconda, but they had reduced its once fertile plains to the scorched, barren state Peri and Hugo had earlier seen for themselves.

If so few gastropods could cause so much damage, it would take very little time to devour any produce grown on the two planets Mestor wished to cultivate. Yet only a few metres from them were millions of eggs awaiting the opportunity to hatch. Simple mathematics had told the Doctor that three small planets could not support so many hungry, greedy mouths. Therefore, he had concluded, Mestor's intention must be to extend his empire a great deal further.

So how best to do this?

As far as the Doctor knew, Mestor was not involved in building a massive fleet of transporters, but he was interested in moving planets. One very effective way to distribute his unhatched eggs would be to create an enormous explosion. The easiest way to create the tremendous power necessary would be to explode a star. And the simplest way to do that would be to send a hard, cold, massive rock spinning to its heart.

In fact, a planet would do very nicely.

When the Doctor had subsequently discovered that the shell of the gastropod eggs could resist the maximum setting on a laser cutter – some ten thousand degrees centigrade – without incurring a scratch, Mestor's scheme seemed obvious. Domination of the universe with his own kind by exploding the Jacondan sun.

Such were the brutal, murderous implications of what was intended, that on completion of relating these facts, the Doctor wasn't certain he could believe them himself. But the sad, nodding head of Azmael confirmed he had come to the same conclusion.

The shocked silence of the group was broken by the squeaky, outraged voice of the twins. 'Mestor expected us to achieve that for him!'

The Doctor concurred.

'Outrageous!' stamped Romulus.

'Our genius was to be abused,' echoed his sibling.

But the Doctor was no longer listening. Instead of petty complaints what was needed now was a plan of action.

'Hugo,' ordered the Doctor. 'You must escort the twins and Peri back to the safety of the TARDIS. As

Mestor still needs the twins alive, you shouldn't be under any threat of death.'

The young pilot nodded.

'And what do we do?' enquired Azmael.

'Deal with Mestor!'

The elderly Time Lord's face crinkled into a half ironic smile. 'Are we capable? Look at us, Doctor. I am old. I have even lost my ability to regenerate . . . And you . . . Your mind could cloud at any moment. We are hardly fit competition for someone with the power that Mestor controls.'

'Better we die in harness, battling against the odds, than die in fear, finding menace in our own shadow. We have spent our lives fighting evil. We are certainly too old to give up that particular habit now.'

The Doctor's words sounded bold and exciting to Azmael. To die fighting evil was a romantic notion he had always held, but he was also aware of Mestor's skill at humiliating his victims before death.

There was little honour or romantic bravado in being nailed to a tree with your eyes put out, your tongue missing and the skin flailed from your body.

Still, thought Azmael, there was even less honour in dying afraid of a knock on the door or being scared of going out after dark.

He had vowed to destroy Mestor and now was his chance. With the Doctor at his side, he stood a greater opportunity of succeeding. And with the knowledge of Mestor's ambition numbing his sensibilities, he was provided with a greater and more honourable motive than simple, petty revenge.

'I'm with you, Doctor!'

'Good man!'

The Doctor then turned to Drak. As he started to

order him to go with the others to the TARDIS, he became aware of the blank, glassy-eyed look on his face. 'Are you all right?'

Instead of a reply, the Jacondan crashed to the floor.

Quickly, Azmael was at his side. It required minimal examination to establish Drak was dead, his mind burnt out.

'It must be the work of Mestor,' moaned Azmael plaintively. 'He must have used Drak as a monitoring point to overhear everything we've said.'

'Then Mestor will be expecting us.'

Gently, Azmael closed the dead eyes of the Jacondan. Although they had not been the greatest of friends, Azmael had warmed to Drak, especially since their mission to Earth. He had liked the way he had taken the twins under his wing, caring for them as though they were his own children.

Slowly, the elderly Time Lord stood up. If he had need of it, the death of Drak was yet another reason to destroy Mestor.

As the Doctor and Azmael left the laboratory, the Doctor picked up two small flasks of Mosten acid which he then secreted in one of his deep pockets.

Unlike most acids, Mosten acid doesn't burn or corrode, but ages whatever is immersed in it by a unique process of dehydration.

Professor Vinny Mosten discovered the acid which bears his name quite by chance when on an expedition to the planet Senile Nine. Mosten wasn't a chemist but an archeologist who was visiting the planet to authenticate a recent priceless discovery of Senilian vases and figurines.

When presented with the discovery, Mosten had become immediately suspicious, partly because of the sheer size of the find, but also because of their pristine state. Further investigatin found the vases and statues not what they were supposed to be, but modern copies, carefully aged.

Further investigation showed the reason for the deception: the planet was bankrupt. It had been the intention of the Senilians to pass off the discovery as authentic, selling the pieces to the highest bidder, thereby solving their immediate fiscal problems. They had also planned to 'discover' further items which they would exhibit, creating a tourist industry which would solve their long-term cash flow.

At least, that was the plan.

Mosten was so angered by the deception that he set out to discover how the Senilians had managed to age their pseudo antiques so skilfully.

Such was his determination that it didn't take him long to find the chemist who had invented the acid. With the aid of a massive bribe, he was able to acquire two flasks of the unique liquid. However, whilst travelling to the press conference where he was to publicly expose and denounce the acid, one of the flasks broke in his pocket. Unfortunately for Mosten, he aged and died in seconds. When he arrived at the conference there was nothing left of him but a pile of grey ash.

Fortunately for the planet Senile, the second flask had survived and, on being analysed, was declared a breakthrough in the science of chemistry. No longer would incredibly hard substances such as modern alloys have to be drilled, carefully filed, subjected to controlled explosion or, in more extreme cases, simply left to weather away. With the careful application of the acid, any shape or depth of hole could be created quickly, simply, safely and, more importantly for money-orientated societies, very cheaply.

Although Senile Nine had been denied wealth through tourism, it now grew rich and fat on the production of what became known as Mosten's acid.

The Doctor knew the history of the acid he carried in his pocket, but he was not thinking about it as, with Azmael, he made his way along the corridor. He was more worried by the lack of guards. It made him feel uneasy. Mestor might be all powerful, but even he would take some precautions.

As they waited for the massive steel doors to the throne room to swing electronically open, it was Azmael who supplied an answer to the Doctor's concern.

'If you were Mestor, and you knew that I knew what you planned for this planet, would you want to discuss it in front of Jacondan courtiers and guards? Personally I would think you would prefer to keep it all rather private.'

As they entered the long, dank, sepulchral throne room, it seemed that Azmael was right. Apart from the massive, slobbering form of Mestor, slouched on his throne, the room was empty.

Cautiously, the two Time Lords started the long trek towards their captor. As they walked, Azmael noticed that massive humidifiers had been installed and that each one was saturating the atmosphere with an ultra-fine sheet of water. Everything dripped including the beautiful tapestries which adorned the walls.

But what broke Azmael's heart most of all were the thick layers of petrified mucus which encased the mosaic floor. A thousand years ago it had taken Jacondan artisans ten years to create the fascinating and intricate patterns of the mosaic. Such was its final glory that it it had been declared an ancient wonder of the Trilop Major galaxy.

Now it was ruined, destroyed beyond restoration, and the slobbering mass which sat upon the marble throne before them didn't care at all.

'Long walk,' said the Doctor flippantly. 'And now I'm here, I don't think the sight of you was worth it.'

Mestor moved uneasily in his chair. In spite of his earlier conversation with the Doctor, he was still unaccustomed to being spoken to in such a rude, off-hand manner. 'Control your arrogance, Time Lord,' he rasped.

As the Doctor had only seen and heard Mestor via a hologram projection, he was surprised by the deepness and richness of his voice. Gone was the marked sibilance and slight cackle the hologram had created. Gone, for the time being, was the melodramatic postering and ranting.

Yet none of these small refinements did anything to compensate for meeting Mestor in the flesh. From any point of view, he was disgusting. And what's more, he stank.

The Doctor hoped they could conclude their business as soon as possible and be gone. The throne room wasn't a pleasant place to be.

'Look, Mestor, Azmael and I have worked out what you're up to and it's got to stop!'

The gastropod gave a small, involuntary laugh, then belched. He suddenly found the Doctor amusing. It took courage to threaten Mestor in his own throne room, and the gastropod was mildly titillated by it.

'Are you listening to me, Mestor?'

The gastropod belched again.

'You'd better be!' The Doctor sounded more like a street bully than a Time Lord negotiating with a creature capable of taking over the universe. 'Because I'm not having your sluggy eggs spread all over the place, causing havoc. Do you understand?'

He understood perfectly, but there seemed little point in taking any notice. 'It seems that you are not only mad, but a buffoon, Doctor!'

This didn't please him at all. 'I'm warning you. Will you give up this nonsense?'

'No, Time Lord.'

'Then take the consequences.'

Briskly, the Doctor removed one of the flasks of Mosten acid from his pocket and threw it at Mestor. But he wasn't fast enough. Instantly a blue barrier of energy surrounded the gastropod and the flask smashed harmlessly against it.

As the barrier faded, Mestor growled. 'You think that I would be so vulnerable?'

The Doctor shrugged. What could he say? He had failed.

'I thought, Doctor, that you would be interesting to know. But like so many humanoid life forms, you are totally preoccupied with your own pettiness.'

Carefully Mestor altered his position. He found it difficult to maintain the same posture for long, chairs being unnatural for his body shape.

'I think it's time I dealt with you, Time Lord.'

'Please, Lord Mestor,' pleaded Azmael. 'The Doctor has been ill. His mind is muddled. It's affected his reasoning. I'm sure, with rest, he will learn to appreciate the respect due to you.'

'He has tried to kill me. He must therefore forfeit his own existence.'

While Azmael continued to plead for his friend, the Doctor glanced over his shoulder and wondered whether he could make it to the door before Mestor had time to unveil another of his tricks.

The thought of dying didn't very much appeal to him. But to be murdered by a slug with pretensions way beyond its cabbage patch would be too much.

'I said, Azmael, that the Doctor would cease to exist. I did not say he would die. If I were to kill him, how would I be able to take over his body and mind?'

The Doctor let out an involuntary snigger. '*You* take over *my* mind. It would be like throwing a pebble into a lake. It would sink without trace.'

'*Please*, Doctor. The Lord Mestor is quite capable of doing what he says,' said Azmael.

'A Jacondan mind, perhaps. But I am a Time Lord.'

Mestor laughed loudly, this time without managing to belch. 'Perhaps you would like me to demonstrate how feeble a Time Lord's mind really is?'

As the question was a rhetorical one, Mestor did not wait for an answer. Using nothing but pure thought he operated a control built into the arm of his throne. Suddenly Mestor was shrouded in a green, ethereal light. Then without warning, a vicious, luminous green finger of concentrated energy shot out and locked on to Azmael's forehead.

The elderly Time Lord screamed.

This wasn't what the Doctor had expected. But then Mestor was rarely predictable. That's how he managed to survive.

As the Doctor continued to watch, a small black blob seemed to work its way along the finger of light.

As it reached Azmael's forehead, the blob spread across his face, then slowly it began to permeate the skin. A moment later it was gone. Mestor now resided in Azmael's brain.

As the green light faded, Mestor's body collapsed, lifeless like the skin of a snake when sloughed. Concerned, the Doctor rushed to his friend. 'Are you all right?'

Azmael started to work his mouth up and down, like a ventriloquist's dummy, but nothing came out. When words finally did emerge, it was not Azmael's voice, but Mestor's that he heard.

'Azmael is now my slave. I have taken over his mind.'

'That's not fair. He's an old man.' The words sounded foolish, almost childish, but then the Doctor wasn't used to seeing physical transference of one creature's mind to another.

'I could do the same to you, Doctor.'

'Then prove it!'

The face of Azmael sneered. 'All I need is . . .' but Mestor didn't finish the sentence. Instead his voice faded, Azmael's pained and agonised voice replaced it.

'He's weakening, Doctor. Mestor is attempting to control too much . . . All Jaconda is affected with his thoughts.' Azmael paused, his body heaving with the effort of controlling the unwanted presence in his mind.

'We must mind-link,' insisted the Doctor. 'Together we can destroy him.'

'No!' The voice sounded more agonised than before. 'He will pass to you, and you will be lost.'

'I can contain him.'

'I may be old,' croaked Azmael, 'but my experience in mind control is greater than yours. You must destroy

Mestor's body, otherwise he will attempt to return to it.'

But how?

The Doctor's experience in dissecting two metre long slugs was non-existent, although he did recall having once read that the garden variety could be destroyed by covering them with sodium chloride. But where would he find enough salt?

'Hurry, Doctor!' screamed Azmael. 'I cannot control Mestor for much longer.'

Suddenly the Doctor remembered the second flask of Mosten acid and set about searching for it in his cavernous pockets.

The Doctor was angry with his lapse of memory. He had wasted valuable time. Azmael had been right to warn him against taking on Mestor. In spite of his vast improvement, the Doctor's regeneration was far from complete.

Finding the flask, he moved to the gastropod's moribund carcass and emptied the contents over it.

The response was immediate. Huge blisters began to form on the moist, oily epidermis which then burst, scattering dry clouds of flakey skin. At the same moment, the corpse started to sag and fold in on itself as though a large invisible weight was pressing down on it.

As the dehydration process continued, Mestor's spindly limbs snapped and powdered like old paper exposed to a sudden gust of wind. Then his face dissolved into thick chunks of heavy cardboard which crumbled, yet again, into dust.

A moment later, all that was left of the Lord Mestor was a pile of fine grey dust, not unlike the ash of spent charcoal.

The Doctor turned to Azmael. 'It's done,' he said quietly.

'Too late, Time Lord!' It was voice of Mestor. 'I now completely control your friend's mind.'

But he had spoken too soon.

Suddenly the body of Azmael began to sway, then reel like a drunken man. 'What's happening?' roared Mestor.

There was a pause, then the strained, agonised voice of Azmael was heard. 'You're dying, Mestor. I'm doing the one thing you cannot control – I am regenerating!'

Again, the voice changed and Mestor started to rant and shout.

The Doctor turned away, angered and frustrated that he could do nothing to help. The mortal battle which was taking place inside his friend's mind was one that could only be fought by him alone. To interfere could prove fatal.

As Azmael struggled to stay upright, he staggered and wobbled about the room. But even with the wall as support, the effort proved too much and he collapsed.

Horrified, the Doctor rushed to the crumpled heap. 'You can't regenerate,' he pleaded. 'You've used up your allotted number of lives.'

Summoning the last of his energy, Azmael forced a smile to his lips. 'Do you not think I know that?'

As he spoke, a black, amorphous stain seemed to swirl and spread under the skin of his forehead. For a moment, the Doctor thought his friend was experiencing a massive haemorrhage.

'Do not be afraid at what you see,' said Azmael. 'It is all that remains of Mestor. He is trying to break out, evacuate my dying frame.' The strain grew into a pulsing blob. 'But he won't succeed. I can sense his strength is failing.'

Azmael began to cough tiny specks of blood. 'He is finished.'

Then slowly, almost imperceptively at first, the blob began to shrink. Somewhere, in what sounded like the distant depths of time and space, a ghostly scream was heard. It was Mestor.

'Why did you regenerate?' said the Doctor sadly.

'I had no other choice.'

'We should have mind-linked. Together we could have defeated him.'

Again, Azmael coughed, but this time blood flowed freely from his mouth. 'My friend, you are too unstable. He would have swamped you... *You* would have been the pebble drowning in *his* lake.'

'But to throw away your life...'

Azmael smiled for the last time. 'It was nearly over.' He paused, the effort to talk was proving very painful. 'My only regret,' he panted, 'was leaving Gallifrey when it needed me most... To become a renegade is to give up one's roots...'

The Doctor nodded, knowing only too well how he felt.

'But still, my friend,' the voice was even weaker, 'I did try to do my best for Jaconda...'

Azmael started to cough violently, the rattle of death apparent. The old man was fading fast.

'Jaconda certainly gave me a good life... Many great moments.' The words were separated by violent gasps for air. 'But one of my best... was that time by the fountain... my friend...'

The elderly Time Lord coughed for the last time and died.

The Doctor gazed down at his mentor. He felt sad

and angry. 'I shall miss you, old friend,' he muttered. 'I shall indeed.'

In spite of having the twins as protection, Hugo and Peri had not had an easy time getting to the TARDIS. They had had to contend with Noma and his troop, who in spite of Mestor's strict instruction that the twins were not to be harmed, had attempted some rather unpleasant things.

Slarn, Mestor's senior chamberlain, had been sent to supervise the action, but instead of being a cautionary influence, had become over-excited and added to the mayhem.

But that was now all over. Azmael had been right when he said that all Jaconda was affected by Mestor's thoughts. Now he was dead, and his control relinquished, the Jacondan guards and courtiers seemed to have lost their drive and motivation. Like lost children, they wandered aimlessly around, confused and concerned as to what would happen next.

All except Slarn. As one of Mestor's most trusted advisers, he was only too aware, once his fellow Jacondans had recovered from their temporary disorientation, what would happen to him. He had been too diligent, too enthusiastic to serve his master and in so doing had made a lot of enemies. Knowing that his next appointment would be with an execution squad, Slarn had tried to bribe Peri and Hugo into taking him away from Jaconda in the TARDIS.

With his mission and career in tatters, Hugo had been tempted to try (after all, six million credits is a lot of money), but the memory of the Doctor's warning that it was more difficult to fly the TARDIS than it appeared, had jolted him into caution.

Slarn had then turned to the twins who were convinced that, for the right price, they could mathematically deduce how to operate the time-machine. Such was Slarn's desperation that he entered into negotiation. By the time the Doctor joined them, they had forced up their price, much to Hugo's chagrin, to ten million credits.

The man who returned from witnessing the death of Mestor and Azmael was very different from the one Peri and Hugo had left behind in the laboratory.

Gone was the vague and erratic behaviour. Gone, too, was the false bravado. The Doctor had now fully regenerated.

Peri wondered how the *new* Doctor would behave and whether he would still want her to travel with him.

As the Doctor ordered the Jacondan guards from the TARDIS, she became aware of a colder, more remote manner to the way he spoke.

Wanting to test how cool and emotionless the Doctor had really become, Peri enquired, 'Now Mestor is dead, what about the people of this planet? We can't just leave them.'

'They'll survive. The influence of Mestor is beginning to fade. Some of the Jacondans have already formed themselves into militia groups and are dealing with the gastropods. I think we have little to fear.'

Fortunately, the Doctor gave a little smile before uttering his last sentence. Peri hoped there would prove to be more smiles and less chilly matter-of-fact logic in the man.

'But who will lead the Jacondans now Mestor is dead?' said Hugo.

'Certainly not Azmael.' There was a brief pause, but

Peri wasn't certain whether it was for reasons of grief or effect. Then at last he said, 'Azmael's dead.'

The Time Lord crossed to the console and started to set the co-ordinates for Earth.

'May I stay?' said Hugo. 'I think I could be of some use here.'

'Really?' The Doctor thought he was mad. But then again, he had noticed Lieutenant Hugo Lang metaphorically measuring himself up for the presidency of the planet.

'I've no reason to go back. People on Earth think I'm dead.'

The Doctor knew that Hugo wasn't the stuff heroes were made from, but then there was more to being a good president than being a hero.

He was also aware that the young pilot was lazy and immature. But then, perhaps in striving to become president, he might accelerate his development, for the Jacondans weren't fools and would soon see through hollow promises and misguided leadership. If Hugo Lang thought he could bully and deceive his way to the top, he was mistaken. After Mestor, the Jacondans would be very weary of allowing another despot to rule them.

'Go,' said the Doctor at last. 'And good luck.'

Smiling, Hugo shook everyone's hand and departed.

In many respects the Doctor had been wrong in his assumption. Although Hugo had momentarily considered whether high office would suit him, his heart was set on something far more basic.

Slarn was frightened of being killed. Whatever else Hugo could do, he was good with a gun. And when someone had ten million credits to spend on simple bribery, Hugo was convinced he could earn some of that money by offering to keep Slarn alive.

As the twins explored the TARDIS, thinking the inevitable thought that it was larger inside than out, the Doctor pressed the master control and the time-machine started for Earth.

Peri watched the face of the new Doctor, as he carefully made his way round the console, making final adjustments to the controls. He looked tired and a little sad.

'I'm sorry about Azmael,' she said, sincerely.

'Hollow words,' snapped the Doctor. 'You had no reason to like Azmael.'

Although startled and angered by the aggressive response, Peri was more concerned that he was about to have another of his fits. Even so, she wasn't prepared to allow the Doctor to get away with his unpleasantness. 'I wasn't feeling sorry for Azmael,' she said. 'I was feeling sorry for you.'

The Doctor looked at Peri. 'How can you feel sorry for me? You don't understand how a Gallifreyan experiences grief. Come to that you don't understand me as a person. You don't even *know* me any longer.'

'That's certainly true,' she shouted, giving full vent to the pent-up fury she had felt since the Doctor's regeneration. 'And I don't think I want to, until you take a crash course in manners.'

The Doctor frowned. 'You seem to forget, I am not only from another culture, but also a different planet from you. I am alien. Therefore, I am bound to have different values and customs.'

'Your former self was polite enough.'

'True. But at such a cost. I was on the verge of

becoming neurotic.'

Peri gave up. It was pointless arguing. He had an answer to everything. All she wanted now was to go home and she told the Doctor so.

'Before abandoning me forever,' he said, 'I would suggest you wait a little while. You may well find that my new persona isn't as disagreeable as you think.'

I hope so, she shouted inside her head.

'But whatever else happens, I *am* the new Doctor. This is me whether people like it or not.'

The statement was as bland and as sterile as it sounded.

Peri hoped that she had caught a glimpse of a smile as he uttered it.

If she hadn't, this particular incarnation of the Time Lord would prove to be a very difficult person indeed.

DOCTOR WHO

0426114558	TERRANCE DICKS **Doctor Who and The Abominable Snowmen**	**£1.35**
0426200373	**Doctor Who and The Android Invasion**	**£1.25**
0426201086	**Doctor Who and The Androids of Tara**	**£1.35**
0426116313	IAN MARTER **Doctor Who and The Ark in Space**	**£1.35**
0426201043	TERRANCE DICKS **Doctor Who and The Armageddon Factor**	**£1.50**
0426112954	**Doctor Who and The Auton Invasion**	**£1.50**
0426116747	**Doctor Who and The Brain of Morbius**	**£1.35**
0426110250	**Doctor Who and The Carnival of Monsters**	**£1.35**
042611471X	MALCOLM HULKE **Doctor Who and The Cave Monsters**	**£1.50**
0426117034	TERRANCE DICKS **Doctor Who and The Claws of Axos**	**£1.35**
042620123X	DAVID FISHER **Doctor Who and The Creature from the Pit**	**£1.35**
0426113160	DAVID WHITAKER **Doctor Who and The Crusaders**	**£1.50**
0426200616	BRIAN HAYLES **Doctor Who and The Curse of Peladon**	**£1.50**
0426114639	GERRY DAVIS **Doctor Who and The Cybermen**	**£1.50**
0426113322	BARRY LETTS **Doctor Who and The Daemons**	**£1.50**

Prices are subject to alteration

DOCTOR WHO

0426200330	TERRANCE DICKS **Doctor Who and The Hand of Fear**	£1.35
0426201310	**Doctor Who and The Horns of Nimon**	£1.35
0426200098	**Doctor Who and The Horror of Fang Rock**	£1.35
0426108663	BRIAN HAYLES **Doctor Who and The Ice Warriors**	£1.35
0426200772	**Doctor Who and The Image of the Fendahl**	£1.35
0426200934	TERRANCE DICKS **Doctor Who and The Invasion of Time**	£1.35
0426200543	**Doctor Who and The Invisible Enemy**	£1.35
0426201485	**Doctor Who and The Keeper of Traken**	£1.35
0426201256	PHILIP HINCHCLIFFE **Doctor Who and The Keys of Marinus**	£1.35
0426201477	DAVID FISHER **Doctor Who and The Leisure Hive**	£1.35
0426110412	TERRANCE DICKS **Doctor Who and The Loch Ness Monster**	£1.25
0426201493	CHRISTOPHER H BIDMEAD **Doctor Who – Logopolis**	£1.35
0426118936	PHILIP HINCHCLIFFE **Doctor Who and The Masque of Mandragora**	£1.25
0426201329	TERRANCE DICKS **Doctor Who and The Monster of Peladon**	£1.35

Prices are subject to alteration

DOCTOR WHO

0426116909	**Doctor Who and The Mutants**	£1.35
0426201302	**Doctor Who and The Nightmare of Eden**	£1.35
0426112520	**Doctor Who and The Planet of the Daleks**	£1.35
0426116828	**Doctor Who and The Planet of Evil**	£1.35
0426106555	**Doctor Who and The Planet of the Spiders**	£1.35
0426201019	**Doctor Who and The Power of Kroll**	£1.50
0426116666	**Doctor Who and The Pyramids of Mars**	£1.35
042610997X	**Doctor Who and The Revenge of the Cybermen**	£1.35
0426200926	IAN MARTER **Doctor Who and The Ribos Operation**	£1.50
0426200616	TERRANCE DICKS **Doctor Who and The Robots of Death**	£1.35
042611308X	MALCOLM HULKE **Doctor Who and The Sea Devils**	£1.35
0426116586	PHILIP HINCHCLIFFE **Doctor Who and The Seeds of Doom**	£1.35
0426200497	IAN MARTER **Doctor Who and The Sontaran Experiment**	£1.35
0426110331	MALCOLM HULKE **Doctor Who and The Space War**	£1.35
0426201337	TERRANCE DICKS **Doctor Who and The State of Decay**	£1.35

Prices are subject to alteration